HIT
to
LIVE

THE HIT SERIES
BOOK THREE

NEW YORK TIMES BESTSELLER
MARGARET MCHEYZER

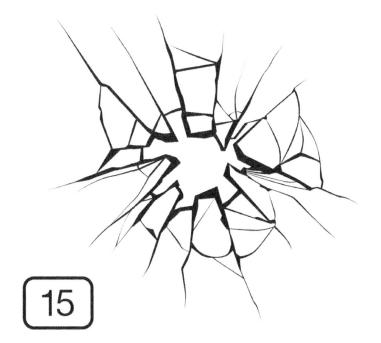

15

Copyright © 2023 by Margaret McHeyzer

All rights reserved.

This book is copyright. Apart from any fair dealing the purposes of private study, research, criticism or review permitted under the *Copyright Act 1968*, no part may be stored or reproduced by any process without prior written permission. Enquiries should be made to the publisher.

Email: hit_149@yahoo.com

info@margaretmcheyzer.com

Hit to Live

Freeze those lemons and use them as weapons.

CHAPTER ONE

ADELE

"Take a seat," FBI Assistant Director Lomax instructs.

"Yes, sir," I say as I take my seat beside Special Agent Tyler Lewis.

Assistant Director Lomax inhales sharply as he keeps an eye on me. Once I'm seated, he returns his attention to the laptop in front of him. "Tell us what you've found out about Ben Pearson," he says without making eye contact with me.

"Ben Pearson is somewhat of an enigma." I notice a few eyebrow lifts and Lomax's lips are pressed into a thin line. I clear my throat and continue, "He's a private person at work. And every advance I've tried in order to gain his trust was shot down. Other than his short relationship with Anna Moore, I haven't been able to get close enough to him. He crosses every *t* and dots every *i*, sir."

The director sits back in his chair and folds his arms in front of his chest. "Impossible," he grumbles. "How can a police chief have no idea about what's possibly one of the largest drug operations in the state's history, happening right under his nose?" I bite on the side of my lower lip and try to steady my nerves. "Not to mention the dirty cop who disappeared into thin air. Are you telling me that you've found out nothing about Ben Pearson, or even what happened to Ethan Martelli?"

"Sir, I've been thinking maybe Anna Moore has something to do with it," Justine, the CIA representative, says.

"Unlikely," Tyler interrupts. "I know Anna was seeing both Ben and Vang, but I don't believe she had or has anything to do with the drugs, and I highly doubt she knows anything about Ben. I spent a lot of time with her while she was seeing Vang. He even subjected her to a polygraph and she passed. I saw the results for myself. I think she was just sleeping with them both."

"Do you think she was playing one off the other? Maybe trying to find information about both?"

"I saw how she was with Vang."

"Perhaps her interest in Vang was aimed toward money."

Tyler shakes his head and lifts his shoulders slowly. "If she was, she hid it well. There was a moment I tried to convince her to leave Vang and she said she knew what she was doing."

"Where's the girl now?" Director Lomax asks as he looks up from his laptop, his glasses perched on the bridge of his nose.

"She and Ben have both disappeared," I say.

"Together?" Director Lomax looks to me, then to Tyler.

"I don't know," I reply honestly.

A collective grumble is heard from around the table. Tyler and I glance at each other. We're both in the shit. "And Vang has disappeared too," Justine adds with a slight tremble in her voice.

Director Lomax pushes back and abruptly stands. He walks over and looks out the window as he crosses his arms in front of his chest. "How the fuck did Vang get bail?" No one replies, leaving a heavy tension pulsating through the room. "So, the head of the Yakuza chapter in this state is free and no one knows where he is? The woman he was screwing, who, incidentally, is the same woman Ben Pearson is screwing, has also disappeared? As has Ben?"

"Um," I say in a small voice. My heart feels like it's in my gut, twisting and churning.

Director Lomax's shoulders tighten as he turns and heads over to the table to grab an unopened bottle of water. He takes a long drink and sets the bottle back on the table. "It appears the woman is at the center of this. Find her, and you'll find the other two." Everyone around the table waits for further instructions from him. "Lewis, get back to the estate and keep your head down. If Vang makes contact, call it in. Let's also put out an APB on the woman. Do we have a current photo?"

"We have her on CCTV from the station," I offer.

"For now, let's keep our interest in Ben quiet until we find him. Put an arrest warrant out for Vang."

"He hasn't missed his court date yet," Tyler stupidly points out.

Director Lomax's brows lift in irritation as he stares at Tyler. "I don't give a fuck. Find the asshole and bring him in. This shitshow needs to be contained before he or Pearson can create any more problems." The protruding vein in Director Lomax's temple pulses faster as his stress rises. "Get the fuck out, and be sure to check in on your designated days." Everyone begins to leave the room, but Director Lomax calls me back. "Petrov, a word."

Knots tighten in my stomach as I close my eyes and lower my head. I gather my courage and turn to face Director Lomax. "Sir?"

"I know we spoke about your mother, and I know you want to find who killed her."

I nod once and wet my lips. "I do, sir."

"Are you able to focus on this case? If you can't keep your head where I need it, I'll remove you from the Pearson case and reassign you to something less stressful."

"No," I say too eagerly. "I mean, I won't let my personal problems interfere with this case, sir. I've already committed to pushing it aside until we have a resolution with Ben."

Lomax sits back in his chair, links his fingers together, and rests them on the back of his neck. He keeps his steely, cautious eyes on me. "If I suspect you're distracted, you're off the case."

"Thank you," I say.

Lomax leans forward in his chair, pushes his glasses further up his nose, and turns his attention to the laptop. This is his way of dismissing me.

I turn and leave the room. Natalia's killer will need to wait. *For now.*

CHAPTER TWO

The hot and humid air jolts me awake. The moment my eyes open, a sickening twist forms in my stomach. My entire body is craving more of the drug I've been forcibly injected with.

The room itself reeks of sour milk, causing a swirl of vomit to sit at the base of my throat. I try to sit up, but my head spins. "Fuck," I grumble as I wipe at the sweat beading on my forehead.

"Get up."

I startle and look around the room to see where the voice is coming from. "Who are you?" There's a fat woman standing by the foot of the bed. I can barely make out her features because my brain is still so hazy. My body screams in pain as I try to comply. I need another hit of heroin in order to comply with her demands.

The fat woman steps toward me and wraps her fat fingers around my wrist. She squeezes as she yanks me to my feet. "Get your whore ass up and down to the office." She shoves me toward the door, forcing me to stumble over my own feet.

I find my footing and turn to stare at her. "Watch yourself," I warn.

A full belly laugh erupts through her gap-toothed mouth. Her eyes widen and her lips form an upturned sneer. "You going to do something about it, whore?"

I grind my teeth together as I stare at her. My head is too cloudy to do anything about it now, but the moment I morph back into my normal self, I'll be happy to show her *exactly* what I'm capable of. "Not yet, but soon."

She grabs me by the shirt and tugs me toward her. She steps to the side so she's now behind me. "That's a good little whore." She thrusts me down the corridor. "I've got your medicine ready for you." My skin tingles with the desire for another taste of heroin. "Then you're gonna get to work, fucking."

"Not a chance," venom spills from my mouth. But my body is weak and I know I hold no power over this fat bitch in my current state.

She snorts with a labored laugh as she continues to push me down the corridor, past other rooms. Some doors to the rooms are closed, but the faint sound of grunting can be heard. I walk past an open door where a woman is sprawled out on the bed. Her head is hanging off the bed and turned toward the door. Her eyes are lifeless, but she blinks once and slowly lifts her hand to beckon me to enter the room. She's wearing cheap red lingerie that's frayed and worn. There's visible bruising covering her arms and legs, along with the telltale signs of track marks.

There's no way she's here voluntarily. She can't even distinguish me from a client. I hate people being exploited for the sake of cash.

The fat-ass devil grabs a fistful of my hair and yanks me away from the door. "I told you to move." My throat burns with a deadly craving for the dirty drug. As she drags me down the stairs, her heavy footsteps make the wood creak beneath her weight. Without releasing my hair, she pulls and then pushes me into an office, where she finally lets go of my hair and waddles around to a desk. "Stand there and don't move, whore."

I'm going to tear her eyes out of her head and shove them down her throat.

She plonks her ass in the chair and takes in a sharp, labored breath before opening a black leather-clad box and taking out a dirty, burnt spoon along with a bag of white powder.

She carefully prepares the heroin and I find myself staring at the magic on the spoon. My mouth waters, and I'm completely mesmerized as I watch her draw the drug into the syringe. I gulp as saliva pools in my mouth.

"What will you do for this?" she asks in a dark and controlled tone.

"Nothing," I answer while staring at the syringe.

"Then you don't get it."

This isn't the place for me to detox. I can't do it here. It's not a safe environment.

As much as I try to fight it, I'm falling prey to this drug. I hate that I want more. I look around the room, trying to break the hypnotic clutch it has over me. I see a framed photo of the fat-ass with a tall, lanky man and a fat kid who resembles her mother.

The door flings open from behind me and the lanky man from the image strolls in. He looks me up and down and licks his lips. "She behaving, love?"

I instantly recognize the voice from Katsuo's, when he sold me.

"The slut thinks she won't suck or fuck cock." The fat-ass devil laughs sarcastically.

"She ain't here to fuck spiders," he replies with his own demonic laugh.

What the hell are they talking about? Fucking spiders? I look around attempting to see what spiders they're talking about.

"She's gonna be a handful," the fat-ass devil replies.

He sidles up behind me, grabs my hips and thrusts against me. "Can I break her in?" Bile instantly rises as I side-glance at this pock-faced, greasy-haired, wimpy-ass fucktard. He digs his fingers into me. "Regulars are gonna love her."

"She's fresh meat and I'm thinking we'll be able to get top dollar for her with our clients who have *special* needs."

"Let me break her in first," he repeats as he grinds his itty-bitty penis against me.

The fat-ass devil lays the syringe on the table and sits back in her seat. She folds her arms in front of her and arches a brow. "We gotta know how she goes." She flicks her hand at him, giving him permission. Sick fuckers.

"Good." He's already loosening his belt while she keeps an eye on me.

This may be my only opportunity to get out of this place. If I can put distance between myself and the drug, I'll figure out a way to get in contact with Agent so he can start the extraction plan. Although I want what's in that syringe, it's the only weapon I have that guarantees me leaving.

As the fucker puts his hands on me, I turn and throw my elbow up into his nose, hearing the satisfying sound of it breaking. I leap over the desk, grab the syringe, and stab it into her eye. Her shrieking echoes throughout the office and undoubtedly through every room in this godforsaken brothel.

The dirty fucker of a husband attempts to restrain me, but with a hard elbow to his gut, I'm able to wind him.

Just as I turn to run, something hard strikes my head and I collapse.

CHAPTER THREE

BEN

"Welcome to Sydney," the female immigration officer says as she waves us over toward her. "Passports." She holds her hand out to Emily and me. "What brings you to Australia?" she asks in her no-nonsense voice as she checks over our passports.

"Karli and I are here on vacation." I smile and casually glance over at Emily.

"Where will you be traveling to?"

"We'll be staying here in Sydney."

The immigration lady looks between us, then back to our fake passports. "Where will you be staying?

"Hang on." Emily takes her phone out of her pocket and looks at the fake email Agent created in case we were asked for specific details. "Um, the Quest Hotel at Potts Point?" Emily looks to the immigration woman. "Did I pronounce that right?"

"You did." The woman relaxes only slightly. "How long are you both in Australia for?"

"We've got our return trip in fifteen days," I reply and offer her a kind smile. Emily and I need to play it cool. Thankfully, we're used to doing that.

"Will you be working while you're here?"

"God, no. This is our dream vacation, we've been talking about this for years, haven't we?" Emily asks as she glances at me.

"How much cash do you have on you?"

Jesus, let us in the fucking country already. "We have a little under three thousand in cash, but we also have our credit cards," I say.

The woman closes our passports and slides them back to us. "Welcome to Australia. Enjoy your stay."

"Thank you," Emily says.

We take our passports and head over to baggage claim along with the rest of the passengers from the flight to wait for our suitcases. There is a heavy police presence in the airport. Some are walking around with sniffer dogs, while other police in teams of two patrol the airport.

Once we have our luggage and are heading outside, my phone rings. "Yeah?" I answer knowing it's Agent.

"I know where she is."

"Where is she?"

The entire time dynamic throws me off. We left the US on Wednesday and have arrived in Sydney on Friday but the flight was only thirteen hours. "She's in a brothel in Sydney. There aren't any cameras in the brothel, so I don't know *how* she is."

"Just make sure Doctor's ready."

"There's a car booked for you under your alias. Hertz car rental."

"What?"

"The car rental company is called Hertz."

I look around and see a sign pointing toward car rentals. "This way," I say to Emily.

"Doctor will be arriving soon too."

I hang up from Agent when I reach the car rental counter. Within moments, we're heading outside to where we've been told the rental will be. "Fuck, it's hot here," I groan to Emily.

"It's the humidity that we're not used to."

We follow the instructions from the car rental lady and find where the cars are. Once we sign some more paperwork, we're shown to the car. The moment we're in the car, I dial Agent. "Where are we going?"

"I'm sending you the address where you'll be staying."

Although I want to break down the door where Anna's being held, I know I can't do that. Not without Doctor's help, because I simply don't know what state she's in. "How far are we from where 15 is?"

"It's in a neighboring suburb." There's a long pause from Agent. "I'll reach out when you arrive at your location. I'm tracking your phone."

We drive over the Harbour Bridge into a residential neighborhood that has an interesting mix of housing. Some old, some restored. We find the house easily and park the car in front of it. "What is this place?" Emily asks once we're out of the car.

"No idea." The house itself appears unkempt and run-down on the outside, though strangely, it fits into the surroundings.

"I didn't come all the way to Australia to be killed by some crazy-ass serial killer holed up in this shithole," Emily says as she points to the house.

"Look." I glance up at the security cameras in the front of the house, then back to Emily. It's then that I notice all the security around the house. The front screen door is thick and made out of some kind of metal. There's a black lock box hanging off the screen door.

My phone rings again, and I answer it as we walk toward the front. "The security code for the lock box is 9-0-3-1-6," Agent says.

I enter the code that unlocks the box. Inside are two keys. They open the front door, and when we step inside, we're instantly aware of the stark contrast to the outside. "What is this place?" I ask as I walk around and take in the crisp, clear lines, and all the upmarket furniture.

"It's a drug dealer's house."

"Great," I say as I shake my head. "So, we can be raided at any moment?"

"The local cops are on his payroll, and he's out of the country at the moment." I rub at my temple as I shake my head. "You're not going to be raided."

"Should I even ask how you found this place?"

"15 knows a lot of people."

I blow out the air stuck in my lungs. "Tell me where she is," I say as I navigate away from the topic of this drug dealer's house and whether we're going to be raided or not.

"The brothel she's being kept in is owned by a husband and wife who have a reputation for allowing their clients to do whatever they want to the girls, for the right price."

"Fuckers," I grumble under my breath.

"They keep the girls drug-dependent. They have some of the local cops on their payroll too. I've got CCTV from around the area, but nothing from the inside. The wife runs the house. Her name is Veronica White, and her husband is Alva. They've got a kid, Chastity, and I hate to say it, Ben, but she's just as bad as her parents. She finds runaways, befriends them, promises a family, but ends up feeding them drugs and gets them hooking."

The hair on the back of my neck stands up as I'm listening to the sickening manipulation of these animals. "Send me the address where 15 is. Emily and I will find a way to get her out."

"There's something I need to tell you."

My shoulders slump forward. "What?"

"Don't get caught, because the FBI have issued an APB for 15 under her alias of Anna Moore."

"What? Why?"

"I'm trying to work that out, but they have an arrest warrant for Vang, too."

I sigh deep into the phone as I pinch the bridge of my nose. "Is there anything out for me?"

"No, not yet."

Yet...

Fuck.

Once this clusterfuck is over with and I've got her out safely, I'm taking her and leaving. She can come kicking and fucking screaming and fight me as much as she wants. We need to make a life together and away from all this bullshit and danger.

It's time we operate as a unit, and not as individuals. I'll fight for her. Anna may have not known my real identity, but it doesn't change the fact that I'll never walk away from her.

And I'm damn well not letting her walk away from me.

Ever.

Chapter Four

Anna

"Wake up!" someone shouts. Ice-cold water is thrown on me, causing me to startle as I struggle to open my eyes.

My head pounds and aches, stemming from where I was struck. "Fuck," I groan as I try to blink the pain away. "Where am I?" My knees burn from an acute pain shooting through my legs while my lower back is tight with a stabbing agony. My shoulders are heavy with a dull ache as I feel myself swaying back and forth. I try to raise my hand to rub at the increasing pressure forming across my temples, but I can't move my hands more than an inch or so. "What the fuck?" I blink several times as I look from side to side, only to find myself on my knees with my arms outstretched and chained to the wall. I move my arms but the rattle of the sturdy chains reminds me that I'm not going anywhere.

I fight the chains again, but this time I'm met with a cynical laugh. "The whore thinks she can get away."

I look over to where the nasally voice originated from. I'm met with the spawn of the fat-ass devil. She's leaning against the wall with her arms crossed in front of her as she watches me. "Let me go and I'll let you live," I say in a low, steady, menacing voice.

She throws her head back and mockingly laughs at me. She pushes off the wall and takes a couple of steps closer to me. "You've caused enough damage, so I'll be keeping you down here." She looks to me and arches a brow while licking her bottom lip. "I have two very special clients coming in for you." She waggles her brow and looks around the room. "I look forward to seeing what's left of you once they're finished."

I pull my shoulders back and lift my chin. "And I look forward to skinning you," I reply with equal venom to my voice.

She snorts sarcastically. "It was bound to happen." She begins slowly pacing back and forth in front of me. "I must admit, I'm definitely intrigued though." Although my body is protesting and in pain, I fight past the physical hurt and keep my eyes firmly planted on her. "We've never had anyone who's caused as much trouble as you." She stops and stands in front of me. "We paid good money for you, and what do you do to repay your debt? You take my mother's eye out and stab my father." I stabbed him? Must've happened during our wrestling. Serves him right; he shouldn't have put his hands on me.

"Lucky it's only one eye she lost. Don't worry, there's still time for me to take the other."

She steps forward and stops just out of my reach. But I know these chains are on to stop me from attacking someone again, which means she's got all the confidence in the world. She rubs her hands together and tilts her head to the side. "You sure are sweet."

"Unlock the chains and I can show you how sweet I am," I say with a slight lip curl.

"Let's see what this pussy tastes like." Abruptly she squats in front of me and shoves her hand inside my panties. She sticks her finger up inside me and wiggles it around. I know I'm in no position to go after her. She's even far enough back that I can't head butt her. She's quite literally at arm's length. "You're not like the other whores here. You're tight, but dry."

She's fucking sick in the head.

She removes her hand to stand and step backward. "Is that it?" I ask with repulsion.

She smirks and shakes her head while licking me off her finger. "You taste like American trash."

"You eat American trash often?" I counter.

She throws her head back and chuckles. She bites her lower lip and arches a brow. "You're gonna be a good little slut. I do hope you like eating pussy, because once our clients are done with you, you'll be eating my cunt." She moves her hand inside her pants and starts getting herself off in front of me. She's watching me watching her. "Do you like what you see, slut?" she moans as she pleasures herself.

She has the upper hand, *for now*.

"For a baby elephant you're alright, I guess."

Her eyes snap open as her hand slows and she removes it from inside her pants. Her jaw tightens and she narrows her eyes at me. Oh, she has a complex about her weight.

Good to know.

She steps forward and viciously backhands me. "You're gonna be fun to break in." Although the hit hurts like fucking hell, I bear down on the pain and slowly turn my head to look at her from below my brows. She's waiting for a reaction, anything that'll give her satisfaction. She's fucked with the wrong person. "I was going to give you some medicine, but now I think I want to wait until our favorite clients arrive."

Fuck, the moment she says the word medicine, my body instantly reacts. I want that heroin, need it to get through this. "How about you shove your medicine up your ass?" I smirk up at her, trying to provoke her enough to give it to me. My mind is still clouded by the filthy drug they've been giving me. I hate myself for wanting it, but I know I'm strong enough that once I'm out of here I'll be able to kick the habit.

But for now, I just need a little to get by.

She steps backward and leans against the wall, crossing her arms in front of her chest. "I know what you're doing, slut." She snickers and graces me with a feverish, evil glare. "And you're not gonna get it. I'm going to let my special client have you as you're detoxing. That'll make it more fun for him." *Fuck.* She pushes off the wall and heads toward the door. "Oh," she says and stops before leaving. "Don't go anywhere before the fun starts."

My mouth is parched and I try to moisten the dryness in the back of my throat. "I'm going to dice you up," I warn as I fight the sweats and shaking.

She stares at me and smiles. Shaking her head, she lifts her shoulders and leaves this dungeon-like room.

I lower my head, letting my chin rest on my chest as I battle the urge for the damn drug.

Ben

"What do you mean a cutter is coming for her?" I ask Agent as I pace back and forth.

"I managed to tap the phones, including the daughter's cell. 15 is causing problems, and the daughter has reached out to one of their *special* clients."

"Who the fuck are these people?" I groan as I run my hand through my hair.

"She took out the eye of the madam who runs the brothel, and she stabbed the madam's husband through the hand."

I can't help but snicker. "I'm amazed they're still alive."

"The only reason they got the drop on her is because they've been doping her up on heroin."

I turn to Emily and stare at her. Her brows draw together and she lifts her hands, silently asking me what's going on. "Tell me about this *client,*" my voice darkens with anger.

"The daughter has delayed him because she said she wants to test 15's boundaries."

"I don't even know what that means. I'm not waiting for Doctor, I'm going to get her right now." Emily's on her feet, ready to back me up.

"No, you can't do that. I'm sorry, but she's worth more than you are, and I'm not giving you any information about where she is until Doctor is here. I have no idea what state she's in, and you attempting to be her knight in shining armor might end up killing you both."

Agent's right. Anna is too important for me to react without thinking. I run my hand through my hair once again as I walk to the back of the house and look out the kitchen door toward the back yard. "Get me everything you know on this cutter guy. Track him down."

"What are you going to do?"

"I'll stop him before he can get to her, and hopefully by then Doctor will have arrived."

"Doctor is en route now," Agent says.

"I can't sit here doing nothing." I close my eyes as I lean my head against the glass pane. I'm met with a long, drawn out, intense silence.

I open my eyes and pull the phone away from my ear to see if Agent has disconnected the call. I see he hasn't.

"I'll find out who this client is," Agent concedes. "But, Ben, we need to be smart about this. We don't need him tipping off the brothel and them moving 15 or giving her a lethal injection."

My throat tightens with the thought of losing Anna. I'll kill every fucker who leads to her premature death. "Yeah."

"I'll let you know when Doctor will arrive." Agent ends the call and I'm left to my own racing mind.

I hear Emily heading toward the kitchen, and I turn as soon as she enters. "What's happening?"

"Anna's being held in a brothel." Emily nods, already knowing everything I've filled her in on. "Doctor is on his way." She keeps nodding. "Anna's being fed heroin to make sure she's compliant, but she's causing problems. She stabbed the madam through the eye with something, and stabbed the madam's husband in the hand."

Emily smirks as her left brow rises. "Your girl is kick-ass," she injects with a hint of humor. "John Wick mixed with James Bond."

"I once called her a female version of James Bond, or a member of Charlie's Angels."

"Except she kills people for money," Emily says.

I chuckle and shake my head once. "That's exactly what she said." The memory is as vivid as if I lived it yesterday.

Emily approaches me and places her hand on my tense shoulder. "I know you want to get in there and get her, but this is bigger than us. We need her back, because we need to take everyone down. Vang, those fuckers holding Anna, and any fucker standing in our way. We can do it on our own, but this needs planning. If you want to go in after her, then I've got your back, brother. But I think we should wait for this Doctor guy too. Because if they've been doping her up, we'll need him to make sure she's safe while she's detoxing."

"I know." I gently pet her hand before she removes it from my shoulder.

"I know you're frustrated, but we can't go in there without a plan or support."

"I know," I repeat. "I just hate waiting because we don't know what's happening to her in there."

Emily doesn't respond. She simply nods and gives me a hug. My mind is filled with dangerous thoughts, and I know if we don't get in there quickly to rescue my girl, I'm going to do something stupid.

I flick a look at the time on the microwave and promise myself that if Doctor doesn't arrive within the next twenty-four hours, then I'm doing this with or without his and Agent's help.

"I'm going to take a shower." Emily breaks her hug and steps backward. "It'll be okay, Ben."

I head back into the family room and sit on the sofa, waiting for anything to happen. I hear the water turn on in the bathroom. I keep looking at my phone, waiting for Agent to call with news.

The moments bleed into one another as I anxiously wait for something to happen. My leg is jittery and restless as I dart my gaze between the front door and my phone.

"Anything?" Emily's voice startles me.

I look behind me to see her dressed in shorts and a t-shirt with a towel wrapped around her hair. "No, not yet."

"It'll be okay."

"I know," my confident reply fools Emily. I'm really not sure if everything is ever going to be okay again. "I'm sorry," I say.

"It's not your fault, Ben," Emily's reply means she knows exactly what I'm apologizing for. "We all knew what we were getting into when our parents left us the business."

"I never should have—"

"Stop it." Emily walks around and sits on the coffee table in front of me. "I'm not angry at you, but Vang..." Her nostrils flare and her jaw tightens. "He's the one to blame, not you."

"I should've—"

"Stop!" She lifts her right hand in a stop gesture. "You can't do this to yourself. We all knew the consequences."

"She was our sister."

"Which is why we're going to fuck Vang up. He and his men took her from us."

"But—"

"For God's sake." Emily abruptly stands and walks toward the opposite end of the room. "I know you're angry and frustrated, but you couldn't have stopped this."

I cast my gaze to the ground. She's right, I'm not responsible, but I'm the head of our family and I should've protected my sisters more than I did. My phone ringing beside me distracts me enough to break the heaviness of what I'm feeling. "Yeah," I answer.

"Doctor will be arriving in the next half hour."

"Good. And the cutter?"

"I've narrowed down who he is, but I need some more time to finalize all the information."

"You have until tonight." I check the time once again, stand, and make my way to the door in anticipation of Doctor.

"I'm having weapons sent to you."

"Good." Agent ends the call and I turn to Emily and pull my shoulders back. "Doctor is on his way." A knowing look passes over her. She knows this is all about to get real. I should give her the option to get out while she can. "This isn't your fight, Emily."

Emily's brows draw in together. "Fuck off," she warns. "We're in this together. We're a family, and when a fucker like Vang takes one of us down, we all go after him."

"This is going to be dangerous."

"Yep." She crosses her arms in front of her chest. "He killed one of us, and we're not going to let him get to another. Anna might not be family yet, but she put her life at risk for you and Claire." Emily moves forward and pokes me in the chest. "For all of us, and we don't leave anyone behind. Get your head in the game, Ben, because if you're going to be all choked up over this, then you're fucking useless to Anna and to me. Either get out of my way, or we do this together."

She's right. I'm letting my feelings cloud my role in this. There's a knock on the door, sooner than I thought. I open it to find Doctor fanning himself with his fedora. "This humidity," he complains.

"Yeah, it's hot."

He pushes through and looks around. "Agent informed me the house is soundproofed, which will make it easier for 15 to detox."

"You've been made aware?"

Doctor turns to me and gives me a once-over. "Of course I've been made aware. I've given Agent a list of things I'll require for 15, and they should be here within the hour." He sees Emily and tips his hat to her. "Emily."

Emily's eyes widen as a small smile tugs at the corners of her lips. "I shouldn't be surprised you know who I am."

"I know what I need to," Doctor replies before continuing to head down the hall, opening the door to each room. He walks into the rooms, then back out, but when he exits the third room, he says, "Yes, this one will suffice. There's a bathroom, and it's darkened."

My phone rings again, and I look at the number. "Agent."

"I didn't need the extra time. I've found everything we need to know about this cutter."

"Which is?"

"His name is Joshua Jamison and he frequents the brothel regularly. A lot of the girls he cuts don't survive."

Sick fucker. "Go on." A lump of disgust rises to the back of my throat.

"He's quite high up in the banking world. He lives in Vaucluse which isn't far from where you are. He's been married for thirteen years and has a daughter and a son."

"Does the wife know about his extracurricular activities?" I don't really want to leave those kids orphaned, but I will if Agent tells me she's okay with what her husband does.

"No, she doesn't." She's safe from me. Joshua isn't though.

"How old are the kids?"

"Ten and eight."

"Is there a sniper rifle in the weapons you're sending?"

"Yeah, and a range of guns," he pauses, then adds, "I know a guy."

Smart-ass. "Send me his home address and his number. Can you keep me up to date with his location? I want to make sure I'm at his house before he arrives. When will the weapons be here?" I double-check in case anything's changed.

"They're on their way now. You should be receiving them within the next half hour."

I like how fast everything is moving. It means I'll get my girl back soon. "Okay, send me this guy's information."

"Already done." I hear a ping on my phone and I hang up from Agent to check.

Emily towel dries her hair as she walks into the room. Doctor is already standing in the family room, waiting on his supplies. "What's the plan?" Emily asks. I go over what I want to do and how I want to do it, both Emily and Doctor nod. "You sure that's what you want to do?"

"It's the only way."

Emily throws the damp towel on the sofa and uses her fingers as a comb to pull her hair back into a ponytail. "I have to admit, it looks that way."

There's a knock on the front door, which Doctor answers. There are two men dressed in suits and sunglasses with two silver suitcases each. "Drop off as per instructions from Agent." I suppress a chuckle, because even halfway across the world, 15 and Agent still carry clout.

Doctor doesn't need any more instructions. He steps back, giving them a wide berth into the room. They both walk in, settle the four suitcases on the floor, and leave without another word. They simply vanish as quickly as they appeared.

Emily opens the cases and leaves them on the floor. "Nice." She lifts a sniper rifle. "Modified." She assembles the rifle easily while I look through one of the other bags. Each of the silver cases has at least four weapons with enough rounds to take down a small army. The only case that has one weapon is the one with the sniper rifle. Emily looks up from the floor once the rifle is assembled. "We'll get her back, then we'll go after Vang." She holds the rifle menacingly.

"First, I'm going to pay a visit to our friend the cutter."

"Cutter?" Doctor asks.

"The brothel has a client who likes to play with knives, and he likes to cut the girls. Most die, but some survive," Emily fills him in.

"I can give you a lethal dosage of something for him," Doctor offers with an emotionless expression.

"I've got it," I reply.

"Let's get to work," Emily says as she puts together the armory we require for my visit to Mr. Jamison.

"Can you hear me?" I ask as I sit in the car waiting for the cutter to arrive home.

"Clearly," Emily replies. "Get him in front of the gates to his house."

I flick a look at his house, then in the mirror. I'm being cautious of my surroundings. My phone rings, and my earpiece picks up the call. "Talk to me."

"He's on his way to you. He's driving a Volvo with the following tags." He sends me a picture of the tags of the car. "He should be turning the corner in sixty seconds."

I roll my car to block his driveway, then turn it off and get out to lean against his gate. "He's turning into his street now," Agent says.

I touch the earpiece and call Emily. "I'm ready," she confirms.

I see his car slowing as he approaches his home. He stops when he sees my car blocking his driveway. He rolls down his window and calls toward me, "Is that your car?" I tilt my head to the side and give him a blank look that makes me appear like I don't understand what he's saying. "Mate, is that your car?" he repeats.

I take my phone out of my pocket and pretend like I'm scrolling through it. "You got him?" I whisper.

"I do but it's not clean because he's in the car. Get him out and move him toward you."

"Can you move your car, buddy?" he says with more force and irritation. I turn and lift my shoulders in question. It works because within a few seconds, his door opens and his tall frame approaches me. "Hey, don't you understand English? Move your fucking car." He points to the car again.

"Got him," Emily says.

"Move your damn car. Fucking tourists, learn fucking English before you come to my country," he says as he gets in my face. I grab his forearm and twist it behind his back, pushing him up against the gate of his house. "What the fuck?"

"Your visit to the brothel has been rescheduled."

"What? I don't know what you're talking about," he says with a shaky voice.

"You sure you want to play this game with me?"

"Look, man, I don't know who you are, and I don't know what you're talking about."

"Your wife is arriving home soon with your son and daughter. Maybe it's your wife who frequents the brothel to cut whores. I can wait for her."

"What? I don't know what you're talking about," he attempts to argue.

"Go ahead," I say to Emily. A single shot is heard echoing through the streets of Sydney. One single shot can easily be disguised as a car backfire. The bullet tears through the front tire of his car. "The next one will be aimed at your daughter."

"Shit!" he squeals in horror. "Alright, alright. Yeah, they put me off for a few days, I don't know why."

"Call them right now and tell them you'll pay whatever they want to meet with the girl tonight."

"I can't. The bitch who runs the place told me something else is in store for the American before I can have her."

"Make the call, and you'd best be convincing. I wouldn't want to leave your son an only child." I wouldn't hurt the kid, but I'd hurt him.

"Just leave her alone."

"Call." I loosen my grip on him enough for him to grab his phone. "Fuck around, and I'll blow your fucking daughter's head off in front of you."

His eyes are red and filled with tears. He wets his lips and takes his phone out of his pocket. He dials the number and looks up to me, then down to the sidewalk. "It's me," he starts. "I know what you told me, but, I'm really eager for this. Give me a number to make it happen tonight." He listens for a few seconds before lifting his brows. "Fifty? You can't be serious, I've never paid fifty for a girl before."

"Go ahead."

The sound of another bullet echoes through the quiet street, and it hits the rear tire of the car. "Fuck," he grumbles, startled. "Fine, I'll be there at..." He looks to me and mouths the number seven. "I'll be there at seven. But I don't want her touched. For fifty thousand, I want her beautiful skin unmarked." His voice smolders with an obscene, passionate hunger. It makes my stomach curdle with repulsion. He closes his eyes and licks his lips. "I want her untouched," he repeats. He's being swept up in the moment and, I feel like giving Emily the go-ahead to put a bullet through his skull. His hand slowly lowers as he takes short, rapid breaths. The guy is getting off on just the thought of what he wants to do to my girl. He opens his eyes and glances over to me. "I did what you wanted, now leave."

I clap a hand onto his back and shake my head. "Phone." I hold my hand out, and he grumbles as he slaps it onto my palm. "Now get in my car."

"That's not part of the deal."

"This isn't a negotiation. You either comply or my partner kills your kids and wife in front of you. But the shooter likes them young. Like *real* young," I reiterate. "And doesn't care if it's a boy or girl."

"You're a sick fucker. If you hurt one hair on their heads—"

"You're not in a position to issue ultimatums. Now, move your car down the street where your wife won't see it."

"It's got two flat tires," he argues.

"You better make it work, *Joshua*," I say his name as if it's poison in my mouth. "Watch him and if he tries to get away, splatter his head all over his fancy car," I instruct Emily.

"Happily, boss."

Jamison moves his car and I roll up behind him in mine. He knows there are other eyes on him, and he heard me give Emily the go-ahead to kill him if he tries to run. But he doesn't. He maneuvers his car down a side street and leaves it there. He heads back to me and slides into the passenger side. "Now what?" he asks as he looks around the car.

"We wait until it's time for your meeting. But for now, I need a coffee." I roll down to the meeting point, where Emily runs over and gets into the car.

"You're a chick?" Jamison howls with repulsion. He looks to me and rolls his eyes. "A fucking chick? Really? I was worried about a *woman*?" He makes for the door handle, but Emily launches forward and wraps her arm around his neck. I stop the car, turn, and with all my might smash him in the nose. We all hear the crack followed by his painful wails.

"Try that shit again and I'll use your wife and kids as *my* cutting canvases," Emily warns. She releases her grip of his throat and for extra confirmation of her words, she slides her own hunter's knife out of its sheath on her hip and she holds it to his neck. "But I'll start with you, and let you die knowing your wife and kids will suffer more than you."

"I'm sorry," he bumbles through a sudden outburst of tears. "Please, don't hurt them."

Emily moves the knife to behind his seat pointing toward his lower back. "Make a move, and I'll sever your spinal cord." She pushes the knife into the back of the seat just enough for him to feel its presence.

"Who the hell are you people?"

"We're the family and friend of every female you've sliced and killed, come to collect payment."

"They were nobodies. Street kids who would've ended up dying. No one was ever going to miss them. Thanks to me, I've freed them."

"They never had a choice, and now, neither do you." I keep my eyes fixed forward, still trying to get used to driving on the wrong side of the damned road.

"Where are we going?"

"You don't ask the questions." Emily punches his shoulder.

Jamison groans as the hit pushes him forward. I glimpse at him sideways. I instantly recognize the terror-filled look on his face. "Don't worry, by the time they find you, we'll be long gone."

His brows draw in together and his shoulders slightly fall. "You're going to kill me, aren't you?"

"I have no intentions of killing you." But I can't promise Emily won't. He exhales a ragged sigh as he rubs his palms up and down his dress pants.

"Please, I don't want to die. I'll do anything you want."

"I'm sure these are the same pleas you heard from all the females you've maimed and killed," Emily says.

"I'll stop. I promise. I won't ever do that again."

I flick a look to Emily, and we both know his words are desperate. And a total lie.

I don't care about him. Emily can do whatever she wants with him once we've rescued Anna. But for now, we need him alive and compliant.

CHAPTER FIVE

ANNA

I open my eyes and look around the room. Lukas has been training me to become an assassin for months now. The training has been tedious and taxing. But I'm determined to do it, because the day will come when I'll take Ronan Murphy down. And when I do, I want him to know that it's me, that I'll be able to get to anyone, at any time.

I'm not at the level I need to be yet, but when I am, it won't matter where they hide. I'll find them and destroy them. The harder they try to get away from me, the more pleasure I'll take in killing them.

I really want Ronan Murphy to hide, because I can't wait to tear him apart. One inch of skin at a time.

He killed my father and tried to take me, and nothing is going to stop me from getting to him. *When I'm ready.*

I turn in the bed to stare at the bare brick wall. I tuck my hands under my head and continue staring at the wall. "I love you." A fond memory of Dad telling me that plays in my head.

"I love you too," I whisper.

"This life isn't going to be easy, Anna," he says as if he's sitting on the bed with me, petting my hair.

"He killed you and for that I can't let him live."

"I know."

"I'm sorry." A tear falls from my eye, and I quickly wipe it away.

"Don't be sorry."

"Aren't you ashamed of what I'm becoming?"

Dad chuckles and I turn to look at him sitting on the edge of the bed. "How can I be ashamed of the amazing woman you've become? I'm so proud of you."

"But, I kill people for money."

Dad shrugs as a small smirk pulls at the edge of his lips. "Do you kill kids?"

"God no."

"What about animals?" I sit up in bed and tilt my head to the side. "You're not a psychopath." I laugh out loud. "Okay, maybe you are. But you don't kill for no reason."

"Dad, I'm an assassin."

"A damn good one." He wraps his hands around mine and gently squeezes. "It's a job, and it has to get done."

"You're a cop, you shouldn't be saying that."

Dad throws his head back and laughs. "Not all life is precious, Anna. You know that."

"Seems our client is extremely keen to get his knife into the American trash chained to my wall."

What the fuck?

I blink several times and search the room for my dad. Where is he? He needs to come back. "Dad?" I whisper, breathlessly trying to compose myself.

The evil fucking baby elephant hysterically laughs. "Aw, was the poor little whore having a hallucination? Don't worry, slut, I've got your medicine right here."

The sickly-sweet stench of the heroin cooking on a spoon forces me to clench my eyes shut. No, I don't want that shit. "Get away from me," I warn.

"Or what?" She clicks her tongue and chuckles.

My heart is pounding as a feral desperation forms in the pit of my stomach. I want what she's cooking, but I need to get away from here and detox. Get that shit out of my system.

But I also want to see Dad again. Maybe on my next high?

No, push through it. He's dead. I'll never be able to see him.

Her heavyset footsteps anger me. My teeth grind together as I look up at her from beneath the sweaty hair stuck to my face and neck. "When I kill you, it'll be nice and slow," I say.

She snorts as she holds the syringe between her teeth and produces a tourniquet to wrap around my arm. It doesn't matter how much I struggle against the restraints. They'll win every single time. She smacks the inside of my arm to bring up a vein, and when she gets one, she sinks the needle into my arm.

"No!" I yell, consumed with pain.

Yes, my body happily hums.

"That's it, fight me. The more you fight the better it'll feel as it travels through your veins."

"You'll die by my hand," I warn before I'm overtaken by the poison.

My eyes close as my head lolls forward. Every single muscle relaxes as the poison mixes with my blood. I'm in total ecstasy, lost in a moment of fevered euphoria.

I equally hate and love this moment. I can't wait to get out of here so I can detox, but I'm in love with this floaty feeling.

"Leave us," a male voice instructs.

I can barely manage to open my eyes, not sure what I'm seeing is actually real. "Who are you?" I moan, although I don't know what he heard.

"Listen," he says as he grabs my face between his hands. "Can you hear me?" My head rolls from side to side as I try to focus on the man squatting in front of me. He looks to the door, then back to me. "Can you hear me?"

I try to force my eyes to open, but I'm struggling. I'm not even sure how long I've been here. My knees are killing me, my back is in so much pain. Is there really someone in here with me, or is it the drug fucking with my head again?

"Can you hear me?" Hands grab my shoulders and shake. "Hey, wake up."

"What?" I open my eyes and try to focus on the man in front of me. "Who are you?"

He laces his hand into my hair and moves his face closer to mine. His lips hover over mine. "God, I wish I could watch your beautiful skin turn pink under my knife."

I blink several times trying to push past the high of the drug. I'm tired, yet still floating high. "I'll fucking end you," I warn in a wavering and weak voice.

He smashes his lips to mine and shoves his tongue in my mouth.

I have a spilt second of clarity, and so I bite down on his tongue, causing him to abruptly stop his assault. The strong taste of metal floods my mouth. He pulls back and I can see him wipe at his mouth. "You fucking crazy bitch."

He comes at me, but I manage to headbutt him and send him off course. The drug high takes over again, and I'm pushed into an imaginary place of absolute bliss.

"I should fucking kill you for what you did," he says. Or, I think that's what he said. I'm not even sure he's real. "They're coming for you," his tone drips with venom. The door opens and closes.

I'm left to my own thoughts. A tidal wave of exhaustion overtakes me, and I feel myself drifting into a bleak headspace shrouded in darkness. My rapid breathing slowly evens as my body relaxes against the restraints.

Seconds pass as a cold, black veil envelops me. Moments tick slower. Time stands still. I feel nothing. A fine line of drool escapes my parted, chapped lips as I lose my grip on reality. The only things holding me up are the chains connected to the walls.

"Anna."

My attempt to open my eyes is futile.

"I've got you."

My eyelids flutter as I look at the man in front of me.

I wish it was Ben and not a hallucination. But I know he's not here. It doesn't matter. I'm not going to make it. I can let go now.

The weightlessness and a sense of serenely floating feels like heaven's opened its arms to me.

"Help her!" It sounds like Ben, but Ben's not here.

"15, squeeze my fingers if you can hear me." Oh, the sweet soothing baritone voice of Doctor. Maybe this is a borderland? Somewhere between life and death. Am I stuck in purgatory? "She's not responding."

"What the fuck, help her."

"Move out of my way so I can work."

"What can I do?"

"Get out of my way."

"Ben, let him work," a softer female voice instructs.

How many people are on this floating trip to hell?

"Administering Narcan," Doctor says. "Get him out of the room."

"Ben, you need to let him do what he's paid to do."

"He's not doing enough," Ben replies.

"Get out of my way, son. The longer you refuse to leave, the less time I have to save her. You've done your job. Now it's my turn. This is what I do for 15. I take care of her."

"Ben!" the female voice says louder. "Get out and let Doctor do his thing."

"You don't understand, I love her."

A perfect black velvet curtain envelopes me warmly, and I fall into a deep and welcome oblivion. *Perfection.*

I rub my fingers together and they feel wet and sticky. My body is soaked as it trembles. A hand wipes a cool, wet cloth over my forehead as I struggle to open my eyes. "Please," I beg, writhing in agony. "Please."

"You need to fight it."

"Just a little." Fire snakes its way through my veins over and over again. It tears me to shreds from the inside. The pain is relentless.

"You've been through worse, 15," he says. "Remember the time you were shot and the bullet was lodged only two millimeters from your heart? Any closer and you would've died. Do you remember what happened when you woke?"

My mind blanks as I attempt to fight the pain clawing its way through my entire body. I drift in and out of the darkness with no awareness of the time that passes. I'm vaguely aware of Doctor and Ben sitting with me as they watch me heave through the desperate hunger for the evil drug.

My body is not my own, and this cruel reality is unnerving. It shakes and cries for the drug even as I attempt to purge the poison from my system.

Through the looming, horror-filled moments, I have small glimpses of clarity. Enough for me to make plans to kill the man who bought me, the wife that insisted I whore myself for her profit, and the daughter who encouraged a man to indulge in his gruesome fantasies.

The plans extend to the men who were hurting the little girl in Katsuo's torture chamber.

While my head struggles to find clarity, I continue to make plans.

These fuckers will die by my hand. Their pain will be like nothing they've ever endured before. I'm judge, jury, and executioner. And I'll do it all without a twinge of conscience. They deserve my wrath, and they're going to get it.

The sheer burn of my rage spurs me to get myself clean so I can head back to America and kill those fuckers. But not before I take care of business here.

I shoot up to sitting in bed as my stomach twists and churns in agony. "Here." Doctor shoves a bucket toward me. He holds my hair back as I hurl into the bucket. "You're doing really well."

My body shudders as a quake vibrates through me. The sweat rolling off me feels like I've had a bucket of water thrown over me. The sickly smell coats my skin as a reminder of the drugs that continue to ooze out of me. The wretched odor clings to everything around me. The bed sheets are soaked and serve as a sickly souvenir of how wicked and devasting addiction can be.

I lie back and open my eyes to stare up at the ceiling. The fatigue is fighting me and I let it win this battle. But I'm going to make this my bitch. It won't win. I'm too strong for it to consume me.

The air is saturated with the stale, opiate-tinged stench of sickness. The scent is tricking my brain into craving more of the drug.

You won't win, fucker. I'm too strong for you.

I close my eyes and let the darkness pull me under. Being asleep is easier for me than being awake. *For now.*

"Anna. I'm going to lift you and take you to the bathroom so I can bathe you."

"Okay," I manage to grumble.

I open my eyes to find Ben leaning over me. "I'm going to lift you now." He slides his arms under my knees and beneath my neck.

The pain is immediate. Everywhere he's touching is super sensitive and throbbing with intense pain. "Ahhh," I cry out in agony.

"I've got you." His lips lightly touch my forehead. "I've got you."

The lights in the bathroom are off, and the room is dark and comfortable. Ben sits me on the toilet and lifts my sticky t-shirt over my head, exposing my sensitive skin to the crisp air. A shiver snakes its way from the top of my spine all the way to my toes as the coldness glides across my tingling skin. "I'm cold." I try to wrap my arms around my body to warm me up.

"Let me take your pants off and I'll lift you into the bathtub." I stay huddled on the toilet but allow Ben to help me. Once I'm naked, Ben lifts me again and gently places me in the warm water. I lie back and allow the water to cover me. The warmth soothes my abused and damaged body. "Sit forward."

I lean forward and draw my knees up close to my chest, hugging them against me. "You're really here," I manage to croak.

"I am." He kneels beside the tub and carefully washes my back.

I turn and lean my head on my knees, watching Ben as he cleans my back. "I haven't forgotten."

"I know."

He lied to me. He didn't tell me he's part of the Pace family—an arms dealing syndicate. For that, he'll have to suffer the punishment. "I'm going to kick your ass."

Ben tilts his head to the side as he continues to wash me. "I'd be disappointed if you didn't."

"You lied to me."

"Technically…" I silence him with a stare. "I guess I did," he replies in a smaller voice. "I'll never lie to you again."

"I know," I say. "But I'm still going to kick your ass."

Ben sucks in a deep breath and finally nods his head. A knowing moment of acceptance passes between us. "Just so you know, I love you."

"That ain't gonna save you."

Ben snorts a small chuckle.

Yeah, he knows he's going to have his ass handed to him. I close my eyes and let the slight sloshing of the water relax me as Ben washes my body free of the sickening stench of addiction.

CHAPTER SIX

BEN

Anna's been detoxing for the last twelve days, and although she's doing well, she hasn't completely overcome her addiction. In time, she'll absolutely regain control, but for now, she's grappling with herself.

Doctor's been by Anna's side, caring for her while her body tries to break free from the invisible shackles of the drugs.

I look over my shoulder toward her room when I hear the door open. I stand to my feet and jump over the sofa to get to her. But Doctor leaves her room and sees me approaching. "You need to calm down. I'm looking after her," he says.

"I'm calm." I hold my hands up in surrender. I just want to see my girl. I step backward and head to the sofa again.

Emily walks in from the kitchen and cracks open a soda can. "You realize she'll be angry when she regains her strength and control," she says, referring to my betrayal.

"She's already warned me."

Emily covers her mouth as a cackle escapes. "You're in for a world of pain with her."

"I know," I concede. "I know," I repeat quieter. My phone rings beside me, and I look down at the number. Drawing my brows in together, I answer the call. "Agent?"

"We have trouble."

Of course, he wouldn't be calling me with good news. "What kind of trouble?"

"You."

"Me what?"

"Facial recognition has you at the Sydney airport, and where you hired the car. We need to organize alternative travel for you to leave the country."

"She's not strong enough to leave yet."

"You're going to have to leave her or you won't get out."

"No," I say firmly. "I'm not leaving her."

"You have no other option, other than being arrested in Australia, then being extradited back to the US."

I'm shaking my head, not listening to Agent's logic. "Nope, I'm not going. 15 isn't strong enough to leave, and I'm not leaving her here."

"You're not listening, the FBI knows you're there. I can manipulate the feed for them to think you're on the other side of the country, but that'll only stall them for a couple of days at most."

"You think I have two days?"

"Three at best, maybe even less."

"We'll all be ready to move by then." Hopefully.

"There may be another problem." I rub at my temple as I close my eyes. "The Yakuza is closing in on Vang. He's been located in the Philippines, and they're already searching for him."

Everyone wants that fucker dead, but Anna deserves to be the one to put a nail in his coffin, not them. "Can you get to him? Somehow herd him in a direction where we can intercept him?"

"I have a decent lead on him now, but the Yakuza have deep pockets and an extensive reach," he replies in a voice tinged with skepticism.

"Do what you can and keep me informed." I disconnect the call and stand to my feet. I head into the kitchen and open the fridge.

"What's going on?" Emily asks as she follows me into the kitchen.

"Vang is in the Philippines and the Yakuza are on their way to get to him. And to top this shitshow off," I say as I gesture around this house. "Facial recognition has me identified here and we have a maximum of maybe three days before I'm found."

"*We're* found," Emily corrects. "It's not just you they'll investigate. It's me, and Anna too." She points toward the room where Anna's detoxing.

I twist open a bottle of water and lean against the kitchen counter as I take a large drink. "We don't have a lot of time, and she's not ready to move. But she's going to have to be."

"We'd better get your girlfriend and get the fuck out of here."

I nod once as I avert my eyes, attempting to make sense of this latest clusterfuck. I push off from the counter and head over to Anna's room. I creak it open and look at Anna, lying peacefully on the bed. Doctor is sitting on a chair in the corner reading a book while Anna sleeps. He lifts his head and stares at me from above his glasses. I jerk my head to the side for him to come outside.

Doctor closes his book and places it on the chair, then checks on Anna. He walks out and gently closes the door behind him so she can't hear. "What do you want?" he asks in a flat, unimpressed tone.

"We have three days at most before the Australian police find me. *Us*," I quickly correct as I point toward the door.

"She might not be ready to go in three days."

"She has to be."

"Detoxing isn't an exact science. It might take her another two weeks, or she might be okay in two days. I can't rush this, Ben."

"I know, but if we stay here, we run the risk of all of us being arrested."

Doctor sighs as he shakes his head. "I'll do what I can," he concedes. "But..."

"I know." I clap a hand to his shoulder, which results in Doctor slowly turning his head to look at my hand. Noted. Don't touch Doctor. "I'll sit with her for a while."

"That's my job," he says defensively.

"I'm not taking it away from you. I'm just going to sit with her."

He arches a brow and nods once. "I have some errands to run." Doctor opens the door to the room and takes his hat and wallet before walking past me. "If she's aggressive when she wakes, call me."

I nod and walk in, closing the door before sitting with my girl.

The room has a heavy, thick scent of sweat. Anna's hair is half out of the ponytail she put it up in after her bath. Wisps of hair are stuck to her face while her body is covered with a fine sheen of moisture.

Anna's legs kick a few times as small whimpers of pain escape her lips.

When she settles, I kneel beside the bed and gently move the hair stuck on her face. I trail my hand up and down her arm; the tender movements cause Anna to sigh.

Her eyes open and close several times. "I like that," she says with a raspy voice.

"I'll keep doing it."

"Thirsty."

I look around the room and find her water bottle on the bedside table. Standing, I head around to the other side of the bed, and unscrew the lid. "Here you go." I pop the straw into it and hold it to her lips. Helping Anna's head up, she takes a sip, then collapses back onto the pillow.

"I'll need a shower."

"I'll help you." She's definitely better than she was when we brought her here.

"Where's Doctor?"

"He has some errands to run, so I'm here." I replace the lid and sit the water bottle back on the bedside table. Anna turns over and draws her knees up while she falls back into a light slumber.

I make my way over to the chair and sit again. I pick up Doctor's book and flick through it. Great, a medical journal that's over five hundred pages in length. The book is not something I understand, so I place it down where he left it. Anna's restless and turns over so her back is facing me.

Scooting over, I sit on the floor behind her, snake my hand under her shirt and lightly run my fingertips all over her back. Her restlessness eases and she falls into a deeper sleep. I like this. I like how we are. Although, having Anna nearly comatose isn't my idea of fun. But I do like caring for her.

The creaking of the mattress startles me awake. I open my eyes and see Anna sitting up in bed. She's scrubbing her hand over her face as she tries to rouse herself from sleep. "Hey," I say as I sit forward on the chair and reach out to rub her back. She looks up at me from her now-disheveled hair that's mostly managed to come loose from her ponytail. "You're looking better." The bruising on her face that was quite vibrant is now mellowing to a yellowish hue.

"Why were you asleep on the chair and not on the bed, with me."

"Because at best, you scare the shit out of me," I earnestly reply.

Anna turns to look at me and smirks. "Probably lucky you didn't try to come into my bed. You wouldn't have liked what I'd do to you," her voice, although weak, still holds authority.

"We need to leave in three days."

"Three days?" She draws her brows together as she stares at me. It takes her only a fraction longer than normal before she slightly nods. "I've been found."

"No, I have. Facial recognition has me in Sydney and Agent can only hold them off for a few days." She licks her lips and looks around for something. In true Anna style, she doesn't ask for help but tries to reach across the bed for the water bottle. "I've got it," I say as I jump to my feet and stretch for it. "Here." I open the bottle again and hand it to Anna.

She gulps at the water, and when the contents are nearly gone, she lowers the bottle. "We have three days?"

"At most."

"I'll be ready." She screws the lid onto the bottle and hands it to me. "There's something I need to do before we can leave."

"Something or someone?" She smirks. "How many?" I place the bottle on the floor and stand, offering Anna my arm for support as she stands. She shoos my assistance away and attempts to stand, but she's not strong enough to do it on her own yet. "Let me help."

"No," she replies in haste. "I have two days to get myself back into working order. I can relax once we're out of Australia." She attempts to stand again. This time, Anna's successful, but she's shaky on her legs. However, Anna is a fighter and I doubt the word *quit* is in her vocabulary.

"How many?" I repeat as I stand beside her, with my arms out ready to catch her if she falls.

"Four."

"Four?"

"The madam, her husband, their daughter and the cutter." She shuffles toward the bathroom.

"You have three then."

Anna stops and balances herself. "Three? Which one don't I have to worry about?"

"The cutter."

"What did you do to him?"

"I did to him what he's done to so many girls and women."

Anna runs her hand across the pale skin of her throat and visibly gulps. "You cut him?" She restarts her journey toward the bathroom.

She was so high on heroin she has no idea I caught him with his hand down his pants while running his knife over her skin. Lucky for him he didn't mark her, unlucky for him he was a dirty fucking ass who liked to cut women. "Despite the fact he knew we were coming, he lost himself in the moment."

"Wait..." Anna shakes her head, unsure on what transpired.

"He was helping us."

"Why would he do that?"

"His help was under duress, not because he wanted to. Emily and I made him a deal."

"Your sister is here?"

"Can we get back to Jamison," I say trying to catch her up to the events that have lead us to the present.

"Who's Jamison?"

"The cutter."

She shakes her head slightly as she starts to strip so she can have a shower. "What did you do to him?"

"I slit his throat with the knife he was going to cut you with. Probably the same knife he's used to kill all the other women."

I turn the water on to a tepid heat and hold my hand out for Anna to take as she steps into the oversized shower. She smiles, then nods. "You did good. You've probably saved hundreds of females from being killed and tortured by him." She immerses herself under the stream of water and closes her eyes. "There's no turning back now, Ben. You're in this world and you can never go back to being a police officer."

"I was only ever a cop to help my family business. It was never meant to last."

Anna turns and tilts her face up to the stream of warm water coming out of the rain shower head. "What happened with the brothel owner and her family?"

"Emily knocked out the daughter, but the parents weren't there."

"They weren't there?" Anna's scoffs. "The daughter isn't dead, is she?"

"I had to stop Emily because I knew you'd want the honor." Her lips turn up into a sinister stare. Anna doesn't need to confirm what I already know. She's going to destroy them and nothing will stop her. She winces as she reaches the back of her head to wash her hair. I step forward and reach into the shower to help. She swats my hands away. Damned proud woman. "Let me help you."

"I don't need your help."

I step backward and sigh as I lean against the wall and watch her struggle to wash her hair. "As stubborn as always," I say.

Anna groans again and lowers her arms in frustration. She drops her head and nibbles on her bottom lip. She's deep in thought. "Ben, could you help me?"

Just like my girl. No please or thank you. "That must've hurt," I tease.

"You have no idea how much I hate asking for help." Anna turns so her back is facing me and tilts her head back. "The strong sometimes fall and need a hand to raise them up again."

"You haven't fallen. You've just stumbled." I gently massage her scalp with my fingers, making sure the shampoo is thoroughly rubbed into her hair. Anna exhales a small appreciative groan, and I smile knowing she's enjoying this.

"Why did you lie to me?"

My fingers stall for a second before I continue washing her hair. A long, drawn out silence passes between us. "I knew you were going to ask me this, but I haven't really thought about the answer."

"How about you start by not lying to me."

"I won't," I confirm. "I can't give you more than I'm part of the Pace family empire, and it's not just my story to tell."

Anna reaches out to steady herself on the wall as I rinse the shampoo from her hair. The front of my shirt and jeans are totally soaked. This is messy as fuck. "I would've been angry, but maybe we could've avoided a lot of this. Especially Claire dying."

The tightness in my chest and the pain in the back of my throat reminds me of my own guilt. "I've got two regrets because of my lack of honesty with you. Claire's death and Vang capturing you."

"Vang did what Vang knows how to do. In time, I'll deal with him. But you should be guilt-ridden for what happened to Claire." I swallow the pain and lump in my throat. I can't help but keep my eyes downcast as I try to purge the haunting torment consuming me. "This is what happens when secrets are kept, Ben. The wrong people die." I wince at her words. Anna's right.

My shoulders stiffen with the heaviness of the burden I bear. "I know. I'm sorry for not telling you."

"There's nothing I can do to you that you won't do to yourself." She looks over her shoulder and pointedly looks to the conditioner bottle. "I should know how much guilt and regret can ruin a person."

"Because of your dad?" I ask.

"I watched them kill him," her voice softens. "And they made me the monster I am today."

"You're—"

"Don't say I'm not, because I am. I kill people without hesitation, and now I'm going to kill the madam, her husband and their daughter. I've always been a killer, so I'm going to tear those fuckers apart."

Anna's resilience is something I'm envious of. "How are you feeling?" I ask, directing the conversation away from my own flaws. I rinse out the conditioner and step backward, drying my arms on one of the towels.

"I'll be stronger by tomorrow." She turns the water off and extends her hand for a towel. I hand it to her, and she wraps it around her hair, then I hand her another to cloak her body. "Everything hurts, but I'm pushing past it all." She steps out of the shower, and winds her arms around my torso. "I wasn't sure I was going to be able to survive in that place." Holy shit, Anna's being vulnerable. "I'm grateful you, Emily, Doctor, and Agent were able to find me."

"I would've set the world on fire to find you."

Anna tilts her head up and places a soft kiss to my chin. "I know."

Running my hands up and down her back, I revel in this embrace until she pulls away. Again, in typical Anna style, she breaks the connection quickly. She's not a touchy-feely person, so staying in a hug isn't her way. We open the door to the bathroom and Doctor is stripping the bed. He turns and casts a wary eye over us. "You're looking remarkably better, 15."

"I feel like shit."

Doctor continues making the bed with fresh bed sheets. "You look better than you did when Ben brought you here." Once he finishes with the bed, he turns and points to it. "Sit." Anna moves to sit on the bed in her towels. Doctor feels her neck, checks her arms, then makes a gesture for her to take the towel off.

"Hey," I say in protest and step forward.

"Keep yourself together, Junior," Doctor warns. "Lay on the bed." Anna removes the towel and lies down, naked. I don't like this. Doctor goes over her body from top to bottom. "Good," he says as he checks her over. "These are healing well." He stops at the puncture wounds from where they were doping her up. "Your knees will heal."

"They had me in chains on my knees with my arms outstretched."

"I know, Ben filled me in when he brought you here." He steps back and hands her the towel. "Nothing broken, and your body's been through worse. You'll be fine," he says in his no-nonsense, deep tone. "I've brought you food, because you need to eat. Get dressed." He looks to me and instructs, "Help her."

"I don't need any help," Anna says.

Here we go again, back to her normal self. She might not need my help, but too bad, she's getting it. I lay out a pair of sleep pants and a t-shirt for her, then step back. "Use me to lean on," I say as I kneel and wait for Anna.

"I don't need your help."

I look at her and lift my brows. "Get your ass over here and let me help you."

She huffs once but stands in front of me. "You must be hard of hearing."

"Shut up," I tease. She uses my shoulders to steady herself as she dresses. I notice how breathless she is once she's done. It's going to take her longer than three days to get herself together, but I won't let her do it alone.

There's a knock on the door, and I walk over to open it. "Emily."

"For you." She holds the phone out to me and peeks into the room. "You look better than you did, but you still look like shit."

"Emily," I warn.

"She does."

"I do," Anna confirms. "Emily, right?"

Emily walks into the room and introduces herself to Anna as I answer the call. I step into the hallway. "Hello."

"We have a major problem," Agent says with a tinge of worry.

"What is it?"

"I have no idea how, but they figured out the diversion was exactly that, and they know you're in Sydney. The FBI is executing an extradition order for you, and the Australian Federal Police will be on your doorstep within hours."

I run my hand through my hair and exhale loudly. "What's the time frame?"

"The FBI haven't been able to obtain a judge's sign-off on the extradition order yet."

Familiar with how these things work, I know I have a maximum of a day. "Fuck," I yell as I pace back and forth.

The door to the bedroom opens, and Anna's eyes dart between me and the phone. "What is it?"

"We have a maximum of twenty-four hours before the police are here."

She looks to the phone and holds her hand out. I hand it over and she lifts it to her ear. "What is it?" She listens and nods at whatever Agent is telling her. "Get Ben and Emily out of here, and find me a new location."

"No, we go together because I'm not leaving you again." She silences me with a hard stare. I shake my head as I grind my teeth together. "No, I'm not leaving." I feel like I'm throwing a tantrum, but she needs to get it through her thick head that I'll never abandon her again.

"I'll be ready to move by morning. Make sure they're clear of the country and send me supplies. The new residence needs to be near the brothel." She's gone back to all business. Her body isn't strong enough yet to do this on her own. Doctor isn't a killer, and she can't do any part of this without me. "Understood," she acknowledges before ending the call.

"I'm not leaving you," I say.

"You're a police magnet at the moment, and I'm not strong enough to travel. Agent will keep you and Emily safe, and we'll meet when I'm done with what I have to do here." She turns and walks back into the bedroom.

End of conversation. Do not pass go, do not collect two hundred dollars. What Anna says, goes.

Or so she thinks.

CHAPTER SEVEN

———— ◆ ————

ANNA

Last night's argument was exhausting. I fell asleep within moments, but the overwhelming desire to scour the streets and find a dealer to sell me a taste was strong enough to wake me.

I'm still weak and my body is protesting, but I need to get Ben out of here before the police arrest him and send him back to America. Once he's in police custody, getting him free will be even harder than hiding him.

I stare up at the ceiling as the sound of Doctor's light snoring mingles with my own heart rate. I look over to the window and can see the light peeking in. I sit up in bed which instantly wakes Doctor. "You okay, 15?"

"Yeah, I'm alright." Other than the fact I'm fighting a battle within myself to find heroin and inject it into my veins.

"I'll get you some water." He pushes up out of the chair and stretches. "You look okay."

"I feel it," I lie. I don't want Doctor to worry about me any more than he already does. He chuckles as he walks to the door. "What?"

"You can lie to that boy, but do you forget how many years I've worked for you? You look okay, but you'll be feeling like a train has hit you." I offer him a small smile and turn my head. "Thought so. Now, I'll get you that water."

He opens the door and walks out. The moment the door closes, Ben opens it and enters the room. "How are you feeling?"

"I'm fine." *I feel like a walking zombie.* He sits on the edge of the bed beside me. I intake a deep breath and look over to him. "You need to leave today."

"I'm not leaving you," he says defiantly.

"You're going to get us all killed because you're stubborn. They don't want me, or Doctor or Emily, they want you. *You.*"

He shrugs and shakes his head. "I'm not leaving," he repeats with the same adamant stubbornness he's been showing.

Frustrated, I rub my hand over my eyes. I close them and concentrate on my breathing. "I can handle myself, but I won't be able to look after you too."

Ben stands abruptly and paces back and forth. "I'm not a fucking child, Anna. You don't need to babysit me. I can hold my own too."

I hold my hand up to silence his stubborn rant. I've never had anyone other than the people on my payroll. Agent, Doctor, Cleaner, and the others, all paid by me to do a job. They all know what they have to do in order to keep me alive, and they all have to comply with the demands of my job. My team knows if they cross me, I'll kill them without a moment's hesitation.

But Ben is *choosing* to step into this shitshow with me. He's not here because he's paid to be. "You need to leave," I repeat, then run my tongue over the top of my teeth.

"Nope." I look up at him and clench my hands into fists. He notices and shakes his head. "You're by far the most proficient, cold and calculating person I know. But we need to start working together to take all those fuckers down. Starting with the whorehouse. I'm with you now, and I'm not leaving. Ever."

"You fucking lied to me."

"If you want to revisit this and do it again, then let's do it. It wasn't just my secret to tell. I had to protect my sisters."

"And how's that working out for you?" My words visibly cut him. I probably should say I'm sorry, but if I'm honest, I'm not. "How can I trust you again?"

"I won't lie to you."

"But you did, and I can only go on past behavior."

Ben's own frustration is shining through brilliantly. He pulls his shoulders back and lifts his chin. "I lied to you once." He angrily points at me. "I own my mistakes, and I'll never lie to you again."

"But—"

"Get the fuck over it, Anna. What's done is done. I can't go back and change the past. All I can do is move on to our future. My future is tied with yours, and regardless of how stubborn you are in trying to force me to leave, I'm going to be staying by your side. I'm not fucking going anywhere without you. We. Are. In. This. Together. Get that through your stubborn, hard head."

Finally, he's stepped up to be on par with me. "Good," I say. "I was sick of carrying your fat ass."

Ben's features soften as his lips slightly part and he steps backward, further away from me. "No more lies," he repeats.

"If I let you do this, we need to be completely transparent with each other. You can't be part of my world if you hide shit from me."

"You have my word, I won't ever lie to you again."

"Just know, if you do, I'll kill you myself."

There's a small tremor beneath his left eye. "I understand." I completely believe him. His lie to me in the past was to protect his family, and I would've done the same thing to protect my father. I would've done anything to protect him. "We're in this together."

I blow out the air in my lungs and nod. "Let's get Emily out of here so she's not caught up in all this shit." Ben stands and offers me his hand, which I take and he helps me up. I'm still not ready for this, but I'm going to have to be. We walk out to the kitchen where Doctor sits and Emily is making herself a coffee. "Emily," I say.

She turns and gives me a small smile. "Coffee?" she offers as she extends her hand.

I shake my head. "No, she needs protein and a good breakfast. I'm making you an omelette with a protein shake," Doctor announces. "Sit." He pointedly looks to the table.

I walk over and slide into the seat. "Agent is working on a plan to get you out of the country. When you're back in America, you and your husband need to make your way to my safe house in New York. I'll have Agent give you access to my weapons room once you get there.

If you need anything he'll be able to help you. I need you not to go after Vang, because I'm going to take care of him myself."

Emily's eyes dart over to Ben, then back to me. "Promise me one thing," Emily says.

"What?"

"Make him scream."

I can't help but snicker. She's my type of people. "I'll do you one better. I'll record it and let you watch."

Her lips turn up into a satisfied grin. "Even better."

I pick up my fork and nibble on the omelette Doctor's made for me. My stomach is appreciative, but I've gone for so long without much substance that I know if I have too much, I'll end up being sick. "Drink this." Doctor hands me a thick, almost-solid, shake-looking beverage. "It's a protein shake," he says. "Just drink it."

I haven't even opened my mouth to argue. I sip on the shake, and find it's something I can drink easier than eating the omelette. "You'll stay here in Sydney with Ben and me until we wrap up the brothel."

"Of course," Doctor acknowledges with a nod.

"Do you think you should stay here?" Emily asks Ben.

"We're doing this together," he replies.

Emily's eyes narrow and her lips flatten into a tight, fine line. Ben's eyes widen as he slightly shakes his head at her. There's a silent game of tug-of-war between them. She wants Ben to go with her, and he doesn't want to leave me. They stare at each other for a few seconds, having a wordless exchange.

This makes me laugh. Out loud. They both turn to look at me. "Can you make it any more obvious? Don't worry, Emily, I've tried to get him to leave, even threatened him, but he says he's not going without me."

"He's always been like that. When anyone was hurt, he'd take it upon himself to nurse them back to health."

"Is that what this is?" I ask as I turn to Ben. I can't help but smile.

"No!" he vehemently denies. "God, you two are as bad as each other." His forehead crinkles.

Doctor snickers as he stands and keeps a careful eye on me. "Don't worry, Emily, I promise to return your brother to you. Unless he pisses me off, then I can't guarantee he'll make it out of Australia."

"Hey," Ben protests. "That's not nice."

I lift my shoulders and sip on my shake. "It is what it is."

Emily snorts and looks down at her hands attempting to conceal her laughter. "Have you got any ideas on how you want to deal with the brothel owners?" Ben asks. A blanket of goose bumps trails over my skin. "Shit," he whispers.

"What?" Emily asks.

"That's her *I'm gonna fuck you up* smirk." Ben points to me.

"Now I want to stay and see what you're going to do," Emily says.

"No, you're going home while I have Agent find me some supplies."

"Supplies?" Emily asks as she rubs her hands together. "Guns? Bombs? What are we talking?"

I sip on my shake some more and smirk. "I'm thinking more about rats and scalpels." I look to Doctor.

"I can spare a scalpel or two."

"I only need one, the blunter the better."

"This sounds painful," Emily says.

"Not for me." I arch a brow. "I need to make a call." I look around for the phone, which Ben produces from his pocket. I look to Emily. "Get ready to leave."

"Ben," Agent answers immediately.

"Nope."

"15, it's good to have you back."

"I need some supplies, and I need them today."

"What do you need?" I give Agent the list of what's required, where it has to go, and the time by which I need everything.

This is going to be fun.

The madam, her husband, and their daughter fucked with the wrong person. It's time for the consequences to catch up to them. They'll pay me back for everything they've done, to me and to every other female they've destroyed for money.

15 is going to tear them apart.

Literally.

CHAPTER EIGHT

— • —

ANNA

I watch as Ben and Emily hug just before the car disappears down the street. Emily's being snuck out of the country and back to America.

She's leaving on a chartered plane that's taking off from some small, rural town in the back of butt-fuck nowhere in New South Wales. It's a half-day trip via car and tonight, she'll be on the plane and her way back to the States, with two connecting flights in smaller countries where we can get her in undetected.

This leaves Ben and me exactly eight hours to get into the brothel, take care of the madam and her family, and get on our way out of Australia. Doctor has checked into a hotel and is waiting for the all clear in order for him to leave and go back home too.

Ben and I have gone over the plan countless times, just ironing out any obstacles we could run into.

"Are you ready?" I ask Ben as he checks all the guns in the duffel bags.

"I'm ready," he says as he keeps checking all the magazines. "Are you?" He casts a wary, worried eye over my body.

"I will be." I stand and head toward the bedroom. "I need five minutes."

He gives me a nod and continues checking the guns. I walk into the bedroom and sit on the bed cross-legged. This is going to be hard because I'm nowhere near ready to do this. But, facial recognition has cut my recovery time down, and I need to get this done now or I'll have to come back and take care of them. There's no way in hell I'm going to allow that family to steal air anymore. If I don't do this now, they'll keep hurting girls and women, and I can't have that on my conscience. They die today. All of them and anyone working for them.

I close my eyes and try to center my breath. But my mind is still clouded with desire for a man-made toxin that, up to a number of days ago, was running through my veins.

I need to push past this and focus on what I have to do, not what I want.

Come on, Anna. You've got this.

I do have this. I'm Anna fucking Brookes. 15. The most dangerous assassin in the world. I can take a target out from over five miles. I'm a fucking boss.

A cool calm washes over my body, covering me in goose bumps.

They had choices, and they'd made them. They could've chosen to not inject me with heroin, not to make me an addict. They could've heeded my warnings when I told them to let me go, but they didn't.

And for that, they need to die.

It's time they know who I am and what I'm capable of.

They'll pay the penalty with their lives. But their deaths won't be easy.

My eyes snap open and I take in a sharp breath as resolve creeps through my veins. I'm going to take my time and savor every second of their deaths. The power I once held is flooding back into my veins, my bones, and my entire being.

I take several deep breaths and push up from the bed. Standing, I look around the room as I gather my inner strength. "You've got this," I say to myself.

I leave the room and focus on Ben. He's waiting by the front door with the duffel bags beside him. With tunnel vision, I walk over to him, ball his t-shirt into my closed fists and drag him down until his lips connect with mine.

Ben's momentarily stunned, but it doesn't take him more than a handful of heartbeats before he wraps his arms around me, laying his hand on the small of my back and dragging me closer to him. He groans as I claim him for mine. There's no turning back now. We can never return to the way things were. We're in this together, until our very last breath.

He pulls me closer, melding our bodies into one. He pushes one hand further down, while the other grips my hip in a deliciously painful and enticing way. "More," I moan. I scrape my nails up and down his back. There's a subtle exchange of power between us. Right now, he owns every part of me.

I pull back and run the pad of my thumb over my bottom lip. "Damn," he says with a sexy smirk.

"Come on. We have a job to do." The urgent need for drugs is screaming at me, but my own personal desire to end those fuckers is even louder. "I had to kiss you," I say as I look down to the duffel bags, then back to Ben.

He leans down and picks them up. "I'm glad you did. I've missed you so much."

I stand inside the door for a moment as I check myself mentally. I'll be lying if I say I'm not nervous, for no reason other than the drugs. But I have Ben with me, and he'll help me through if I need it.

Still, my need to end them is greater than my need for the drug.

"Let's go," I say as I turn the handle for the door to leave.

Silently, Ben leads the way to the car, places the bags in the trunk, then slides into the driver's seat. He hands me the earpiece and the phone. I dial Agent, and he answers it immediately. "How are you feeling?"

"Don't go soft on me," I say as Ben navigates the early afternoon traffic.

Agent chuckles. "You're clear to the brothel. I've disconnected their phones and all CCTV around the area is being run on an hour loop. You have plenty of time."

"Good," I say and quickly relay the information to Ben.

"Your friends will be there in exactly two hours and forty-five minutes."

I look around, completely unaware of where I am. It's only when I see the Sydney Harbour Bridge that I recognize we're close. "We're still clear?"

"You are. Also, Emily will be arriving at the hangar in approximately four hours."

She's been traveling for a good part of the day, and Agent's confirmation brings a relief to know she's not been stopped for any reason.

"I'm tracking you, and you're still good. ETA three minutes."

Fuck, my heart feels like it's about to bounce out of my chest. "We're nearly there," Ben confirms Agent's words.

In a blink, Ben parks the car and turns the motor off. "You ready?"

I look at him and nod once. "You go through the front, and I'll go in the back entrance. You know what to do."

A savage and excited grin pulls at his lips. "I sure do." I'm impressed with him liberating his evil side. It's so cathartic to live without the ordinary, mundane rules everyone else obeys. I live by my own rules and no one else's.

Ben fixes the earpiece so we're in constant communication. "Testing," I say and Ben nods. He gives me a knowing wink and smirk before heading toward the front. I disappear around the building and feel sick to my gut when I'm faced with the back entrance. The exact same place I came into this hellhole.

I take a moment to gather my strength, close my eyes and breathe through the vicious, gruesome memories. *I can do this.*

"Ready," I whisper to Ben.

"Going in," he replies in an equally low tone.

My heart rate increases and the blood in my veins pumps faster with excitement. A renewed invigoration overtakes my nerve endings. This is what I'm about.

Taking care of problems when others can't. These people can't be left for law enforcement to deal with, because they've probably got them on the take.

I pull my gun and flatten myself against the old red bricks, waiting for whomever to come out the back.

Thirty-six seconds and the back door flies open. Out comes the one and only baby elephant looking behind her as she busts through the door.

She's greeted with my gun to her head and my smiling face. "So good to see you again," I say with a curt smile.

"Fuck," she breathes a long and defeated sigh. "Are you going to kill me?"

I nudge her back inside with the gun. "Lace your hands together and rest them on the back of your head. Walk to the office."

"Please, please," she begs in a whimper. "I'll do anything you want, please don't kill me."

"Fucking pathetic." I lower the gun to the middle of her back.

"I have money, lots of money."

The pleas of a desperate person. *They'll do anything I want, they can give me all the money they have, they'll promise not to do it again.* Yeah, whatever. It's always the same empty promises. "Keep going." I shove the gun further into her back.

I look up the stairs and down the hallways, making sure none of the working girls come out. More specifically, that there aren't any clients here.

We reach the office and Ben has both the husband and the wife up against the wall with their hands on their heads. "You?" The fat-ass devil skims her one eye up and down my body. "But..."

She's sporting a black eyepatch, and her skinny husband's hand is all bandaged up. Having hurt them brings a smile to my lips. The husband doesn't look as petrified as I was hoping. What a shame; I wonder what I can do about that.

"They'll be here soon," he says with a level of confidence.

I gesture with my gun for the daughter to join her parents. She stands between them and cowers toward the back. "Who are you talking about?"

"Vang. His men will be here soon," he replies with even more confidence. "They want him." He pointedly looks to Ben.

I lift my hand and hit my earpiece. "Did you get that?" I ask Agent.

"The call didn't go through. I disconnected it at the source, and I managed to get a location on the phone they were calling. You also have two hours and thirty minutes before your furry friends arrive. Get a move on, 15."

I touch the earpiece and disconnect the call. I look to Ben and say, "Check out every room and make sure only the girls are here. If there are any clients, you know what to do."

Ben gives me a knowing nod as he exits the room to double-check the brothel. The entrances have been locked, which means no one can enter. It also means no one can leave.

"If you're after money, I'll give you however much you want. I have a lot of money," the devil says. "The safe is over there, fuck it, take it all."

I remain completely stoic. "Sure, open the safe." She waddles over to the safe and enters her code. "If you reach for a gun, I'll blow your daughter's head off." I position myself so I'm shielded, but can still get to the daughter, then the husband, and finally the devil.

She bends to open the safe, then steps backward with the door slightly ajar. "See?" She points to the open safe.

"Get back here."

Ben returns and gives me a nod. "We're good. Although the girls all look like they're out of it."

He points his gun at the trio lined up against the wall. I step backward to the safe and kick it open with my leg. Fuck, there's stacks and stacks of money. It's nearly filled to the brim. Fuckers are exploiting these girls and have no remorse. "How many have died for this?" I use the tip of my shoe to flick a wad of cash out of the safe. All three divert their eyes and refuse to answer. "Thought so," I say as I shake my head in disgust.

The little black box falls out of the safe too. It has an overwhelming pull toward me, because I know exactly what's inside it. My mind screams at me, telling me to hold onto my strength and not succumb to the deadly contents.

"The whore wants a taste," the devil says as she reads the obvious reaction my body is having to the box.

Her words abruptly yank me out of the pit I was fighting to escape. I turn to look at her, and I'm instantly reminded of the days, hours, seconds of torture she put me through. While keeping my hard stare on her, I move my gun to the left and with one shot splatter her husband's head all over the wall and them.

She screams and covers her face; the daughter yells and begins to cry. The daughter falls to her knees cradling her father's disfigured body. Both of them have brains and blood splattered on them. "What am I?" I ask as I watch them both fall into hysteria.

"Who are you?" the devil asks and blinks rapidly at me.

"You may have heard of me before." My skin pebbles with utter excitement and control. I lick my lips and step closer to her. "My name is..." I draw the pause out, building a natural fear inside her. She's in the industry, she would've heard the rumors, the urban legends, the whispers. "15."

The devil's expression falls, her mouth gapes into an *O*, and her shoulders slump. She reaches for her daughter who's still cradling the dead father. "Chastity, darling." The daughter's name is Chastity?

"Yeah, Mum?" she replies between sobs.

Her mouth turns down as she looks to her daughter. "I love you, darling." Good, she knows what I'm capable of.

"Let's get this party started," I say as I signal to Ben to get the daughter.

"Up." Ben shoves his gun toward the daughter.

"Don't hurt her," the devil begs as she throws herself between the daughter and Ben.

Ben lifts his hand and slams the gun into the side of the mother's head. "I said up," he repeats as he grabs the daughter by her shirt and drags her to her feet.

"Don't hurt my mother," Chastity screams at Ben.

I fire another round into the dead husband, causing his body to jerk and forcing both the daughter and the devil to pay attention to me. "Next one goes into your knee." I point the gun down at the daughter's knee. "It'll fucking hurt too."

"Do what she says," the devil mumbles as she clings to her daughter.

"Down to the dungeon," Ben instructs and walks backward while I walk behind them toward the dungeon.

Once we're in the dungeon, we force them toward the chains. "On the floor." I use the gun as an extension of my hand and wave it downward. They both sit on the cold floor. "Lie down next to each other."

"You said you're not going to kill me," Chastity whimpers as she looks to her mother.

"Oh, I'm not." They both lie down. "Arms up over your head, and your legs spread out."

"What are you going to do to us?" the devil asks. "Haven't you done enough already?"

I look to Ben who quickly chains their arms up over their heads, then chains their ankles spread out. "Are you okay here?" Ben stands before me and places his warm hand on the small of my back.

"Perfect."

"I'll go get what you need." Ben leaves the dungeon and I'm left to have fun with these two.

I first slide on a pair of surgical gloves, then take the scalpel out of my cargo pants pocket and flick the lid off. "What are you going to do with that?" the devil asks.

"This?" I hold the scalpel up showing it to the both of them. Fear clings to the stale air in the dungeon. "This?" I repeat as I step closer to them. "I'm going to have so much fun with this."

"We'll do anything you want," the daughter begs, hoping I have a change of heart.

I hold the knife up to see my reflection in the small blade. "P-please," the devil snivels. "Just tell me what we can do to stop this madness. We'll do anything you want."

"Please, I'm so sorry for what we did to you," the daughter pleads.

"You're a woman. Don't you feel terrible for what you're doing to us? You've already killed my husband; isn't that enough?"

My lack of communication is driving them to plead, beg, negotiate and offer anything for their release. I kneel beside Chastity and run my hand tenderly down her tear-streaked face. I angle her face so she's watching me, and I smile at her lovingly. "Please," she whimpers and closes her eyes, continuing to cry.

"Don't hurt her, please, please." I silence the devil with a hard stare that makes her gulp back her fruitless appeals.

I wait until the daughter opens her eyes once more and looks up at me. She's silently begging, pleading for her release. I show her the scalpel, preparing her for the world of hurt I'm about to bring. All her chins quiver with regret. I bring the scalpel to the corner of her eye. She attempts to squint and turn her head, but I grab her face and forcefully turn it back to me. Without saying a word, I stare at her and lift my brows. "I'm sorry."

I bring the scalpel to the corner of her eye and slice it through her skin to the corner of her mouth. Her screams of pain drive me to continue.

"Stop!" her mother shrieks in an unbearably high, shrill voice.

The next incision is the length of her leg thorough her jeans. The more I cut, the blunter the knife becomes, meaning it's going to hurt like fuck slicing through skin.

The daughter's screams are sending me into a frenzied love for what I do. There's nothing better than hearing these fuckers beg, cry, and plead for their lives. Especially after everything they've done not only to me, but to countless others.

Ben enters the dungeon carrying two space heaters. "I can hear the yelling upstairs. It's muffled, but it can still be heard." He places the space heaters next to each other. "Do you want me to gag them?"

I look over to him and wink once. There's a hum of satisfaction running through me. I know my silence is sending both the mother and daughter crazy. They're probably wondering if there's anything they can do to stop this, but truth be told, there isn't. There's no salvation for them now.

"Okay then, I'll gag them." He leaves the room again searching for something to shut them up.

"Why does Vang want him?" I point toward the door.

"He didn't tell us. He just gave us a phone number and said if he showed up that we need to call his men." He's most likely after me, not Ben and has figured Ben would come to rescue me. Vang needs to die.

"How many of the girls are here because they want to be as opposed to you trafficking them?" She looks away giving me the answer I suspected.

It takes all my willpower not to slice her throat right here. But I want them both to suffer like the torture they've put every one of these girls through. I want them to be awake as death slowly pads its way over them, sucking and nibbling the life out of them. I want them to watch each other die. Slowly and painfully. It's the least they deserve. I just wish I had time to draw this out for days, weeks, *months.*

"I told you both to let me go and I'd make your deaths quick, and you didn't. Now, you both pay the price." I continue removing the clothes from the daughter from the waist down. Once I'm done with the daughter and she's completely exposed, I turn to the mother. She's wearing leggings, so the blade slices easily through them, catching skin on the way.

"I'll give you anything," the mother makes a last-ditch effort to convince me to stop.

"Anything?" I ask, giving her false hope.

"Yes, anything. Let us live."

"I told you, I'm not going to kill you. I've already said that. I'm a woman of my word."

"Then why are you doing this?"

"You've made a living taking girls and women, doping them until they can't think straight, and forcing them into this life so you can make money off of them. I'm doing this for each and every female you've treated that way. I'm their voice. I'm their executioner." I kneel between Chastity's open legs and run the scalpel down her legs. A moment later, her legs begin to look like they've been shredded with fine bleeding lines. I move to her vagina, cutting her labia, clitoris and then down to her anus.

Her screams are the most hypnotic I've heard in a long time. Not as sweet as what Katsuo's will be though, I imagine. I can't wait until I get my hands on him.

"Stop!" the mother screams. "You're hurting her."

Ben enters the dungeon and shoves something into the mother's mouth and tapes it over. He repeats the process with the daughter, muffling both their cries and screams.

"Time?" I ask Ben as I move to replicate the same cuts on the mother.

They've made a living on selling these girls to sex, so it's only natural, that I take their lives the same way.

"You have fifteen minutes before our guests arrive." Ben stands back and watches me work. At no point does he move to stop me. Once the mother is cut up, I stand and back away.

"This has been fun," I say as I take my gloves off.

The daughter is now just whimpering as the mother's cries of pain ease into sobbing. I gesture to Ben for the space heaters. He makes quick work at plugging them in and turning them on.

Both women's chests are heaving quickly as tears cling to their cheeks. I walk over to the duffel bag Ben brought into the dungeon, kneel and line up the bottles of water. Both the women are watching me intently. They have no idea how much fun I'm having. My earpiece rings and I touch it to answer. "The rats will be there any minute."

I look to Ben, then the two women. I unclasp the lids of the water bottles and pick two up. Ben takes the other two and follows behind me. I stand between the two women and begin to tip the water over the lower, exposed part of their bodies. They scream and writhe on the cold, dirty dungeon floor. The same dungeon where they had me on my knees and chained. I'm sure this dungeon has seen many deaths. What are two more to add to it?

"You'll think of me while you're being dealt the last of your punishment. Every single moment you suffer, my name will be on your lips." I smile as I take the two bottles from Ben and tip them over the women. "We'll call the authorities in two hours, and if you're still alive and want to come after me to settle the score, I'll be waiting. If not, I'll see you in hell."

I step backward through the puddles of water and blood mixed around their bodies. The space heaters are making the room unbearably hot and humid. Ben looks around the room. He takes my gloves, the scalpel, and the duffel and makes his way to the door. I follow behind him, hearing the two women crying and attempting to get free of their restraints.

Ben and I make our way out the back entrance as a white van pulls up outside. Agent's timing is flawless, as usual.

A man in gray overalls gets out of the van and opens the sliding door. "You called for brown rats." He's shady as fuck, and doesn't even look around suspiciously. This guy has done dirty things in the past, and he clearly asks no questions.

"I'll take them," Ben says.

There are numerous cages and containers housing all kinds of animals in the back of the van. The man slides two cages out and starts to lift them. "We'll take it from here," I say.

The guy shrugs and steps to the side. He pulls out a pack of cigarettes and lights one while Ben takes the cages and disappears back inside the brothel. It doesn't take him long before he emerges with two empty cages. The waiting guy grabs the cages and slides them back into the van, all while still smoking. He gets back into the van without uttering another word and leaves, like nothing has happened.

"Why tip the water over them?" Ben asks as we make our way back to the car.

"Brown rats can't survive in heat without water. It's hot in there. So they'll gnaw at anything to get water."

A shudder tears through Ben's body. "You scare the shit out of me sometimes."

"Well, they fucked with the wrong person."

We get into the car and I touch my earpiece to connect with Agent. "How did it go?"

"I think the rats have a lot to eat."

"Ewww," Agent grumbles.

"We're on the way to dump everything, then we'll be at the hotel."

"I'll be watching to make sure you're in the clear. You have the dump point?"

"We do," I reply. The call ends as Ben and I make our way down to a deserted beach. There's always a risk of having people around, or worse, cops. But seeing as it's late and dark, I doubt many people will be around now. We're still careful. When we find the perfect spot, we dump both of the duffels and keep the backpack with the money from the brothel that Ben collected when he was searching for the space heaters.

The drive back to the hotel is easy, although navigating Sydney streets where they drive on the opposite side of the road is another thing entirely. We park the car and head up to the hotel. I call Agent as we enter the hotel. "I see you," he says. "Turn left and walk down the corridor."

I link my hand with Ben's and follow Agent's instructions. "Got it."

"There's a camera on the left." I tilt my head to the right, and Ben instinctually follows what I'm doing without being prompted. "Okay, you're good. Follow it to the end and turn left." We keep going. "Camera on the left again." I look to the right, as does Ben.

"Third door on the right." Doctor is already waiting with the door open for us. Ben and I duck in, and Doctor closes the door.

I touch the earpiece and disconnect the call.

"Any problems?" Doctor asks as he quickly assesses me.

"Not at all. But Ben and I need to take a shower and you need to dispose of our clothes."

"I'm not Cleaner," he says in a grumpy and clipped tone. He pointedly looks toward a suitcase. "From Agent."

"You'll dispose of these clothes when we take a shower."

"What do you want me to do with them?"

"Get rid of them, and make sure they stay gone."

He nods and intakes a sharp breath. "What happens now?"

"You'll fly out tomorrow." He darts his eyes around the room as he visibly swallows. "Ben, empty the money on the bed, then strip. I need all your clothes and shoes." Ben proceeds to do as I've instructed while I strip down to my underwear. I shove our clothes into the backpack, then hand it to Doctor. Ben heads into the bathroom. "Find a spot around the wharf and drop the bag in. Weigh it down with anything heavy."

"Oh, hang on." Doctor opens the mini fridge in the room and fills the backpack with cans of soda and bottles of beer. "This should weigh it down enough." He holds it out to me for my approval. I give him a nod and hand it back to him. Doctor dons his fedora and walks over to the door with the backpack. "I'll be back in an hour."

"Make it two," I say.

Doctor rolls his eyes and huffs slightly. He walks out of the hotel room, and I head straight into the bathroom where Ben's lips are already on me. "I've missed you," he whispers as he claims me with his mouth.

"I need to be fucked, Ben."

He takes both my hands in his and lifts them over my head. I hook my leg over his hip and push my groin into his. Ben's erection feels delicious against me. He yanks my panties to the side and sinks his hard cock into me. "Jesus," he groans. His hot breath mingles with my own as his mouth ravages mine.

He painfully grips my hip, digging his fingers into my still-tender skin. "Harder," I moan against his mouth. I'm deprived and hungry, I need more.

He falls to his knees, hooks my leg over his shoulder, and savages me with his mouth and tongue. "Delicious." He curls his tongue inside of me before pulling back and paying particular attention to my clit.

I scrape my fingers through Ben's scalp and pull him closer to where I want his mouth and tongue. For a split second, the thought of getting a hit of heroin pulls me away from the immense pleasure I'm experiencing at the moment.

I close my eyes as I guide Ben's head, holding him closer as I near my own release. I need this. No, need isn't a strong enough word. It's more than need, more than a desire, more than...anything.

Ben expertly plays my body, using his mouth and fingers to bring me to a quivering mess. "Ben," I groan as my body takes over and shivers around his mouth. "No more." I try to push his head away, but Ben adamantly stays put and continues to lap at me, drinking me like a thirsty man in the desert. After my body shivers again with a second orgasm, he stands, hooks my leg around his hip, and impales me on his hard cock. He thrusts into me as I squeeze my pussy around his cock.

"That's it, baby. Give me more of that." His strong arms hold me up as he keeps smashing into me. "I've got you." I know he does. "Squeeze that tight cunt around my cock, baby." I tense every muscle for as long as I can as he drives into me over and over again. He moves his hand down between us and flicks my clit. "Come on me." His thumb applies pressure while he twirls it around and around.

"I can't," I whisper, absolutely spent.

"One more. Give it to me. I want it." He speeds up, both in his thrusting and his fingering of my clit. Like a damn puppet, I explode around his cock once again. Shivering with desire, I hold onto Ben as my body quakes. "I've got you," he whispers as he pumps only a few more times before he releases.

I stay wrapped around Ben for a long moment before he kisses my forehead. "I..." I'm not even sure what to say.

"I know," he says and pulls out of me. "We need to shower and get ready to go."

That's not what I was going to say. I lower my chin for a moment so I can gather my thoughts. "I didn't think the day was going to end with this, or with us sneaking out of the country."

Ben walks over to the shower and turns it on. The massive rain shower head is ample to accommodate us both. "Nor did I think I'd love watching you torture that mother and daughter."

"You enjoyed that?" I ask as I step into the shower.

He smirks and glances to the wall at the side. "You're amazing," he says. "I've always known that, but watching you in your element is like nothing I've ever seen before."

"I was torturing them." Ben squeezes some liquid soap into his hands, foams it up, and begins to wash my body, paying special attention to my breasts. "Are you enjoying that?"

"I find myself in a predicament, Anna."

"Why's that?"

"Because I think I'm more like you than I ever thought. I really did enjoy watching you work. I had no interest in the gruesome part, but I liked helping you."

"Maybe you're more fucked up than you thought," I say as I turn and let him wash my back and ass.

"I think I am. And, I'm okay with that."

I turn again and wrap my arms around his neck. "There'll come a time when the screams will haunt you."

"Did that happen to you?"

"There's only one person who still haunts me to this very day."

"Your father," Ben says with confidence. I nod and place a small kiss on his mouth. "And what do you do when your father haunts you?"

I pull back and nibble on my lower lip, painfully aware of Ben carefully watching. In this moment, I have a decision to make. I can scour the streets and find someone who can sell me heroin so I forget about the look my father had on his face when they killed him, or I can remember how I've put a bullet in the head of every fucker who benefited from killing my father.

I might be an assassin, but I take care of trash when no one else can.

"I remind myself that the scum I kill deserve to die."

"An executioner for hire," Ben says. I look up at him and nod. "One who has morals."

"I'm a bad person, Ben. I don't pretend that I'm not. You saw how easy it was for me to kill and torture those back at the brothel. They were nothing to me. Just trash that needed to be taken care of."

"Because they were nothing."

"That's what I do when my father's death haunts me. I remind myself of all the people I've killed who deserved it."

He steps forward and embraces me against his hard, wet body. "And I can't wait to see more of your work."

Yep, this confirms it. Ben is as fucked up as I am.

Good.

CHAPTER NINE

MYSTERY

For years I've watched her and let her forge her own way forward. She's never needed me, nor would I have interfered. She's the toughest woman I've ever known. Hell, she's harder than most men I know.

Her sister is tough too, though she's taken the wrong path. Although I love her, I'm disappointed in her.

I want them to finally meet, and to know the other exists. Perhaps they'll find a way to work together.

The boy is a good companion for her, and I know he'll look after her. He's good at holding secrets, as he did for such a long time with his own family.

My girls are tough though, and they can stand on their own feet without needing a man.

I need to herd them in the same direction so they can finally meet.

But first, I need to find out where the main link is. Katsuo Vang. When I find where he is, I'll leak it to the FBI. That way, her people will find out and send her to finish him.

I'm looking forward to seeing what she does to him. I really do enjoy reading about and seeing the images of her handiwork.

My hope is for them to work together. To take their rightful places. There's no one else I trust to do this.

No one comes close.

Only my girls are the rightful heirs to the legacy.

CHAPTER TEN

ANNA

I sit on the edge of the bed, dressed in the clothes Agent had sent over. I fix my hair before slipping my feet into the sneakers and tying the shoelaces.

"How are you feeling?" Ben asks.

"Fucked." I smirk up at him as he finishes getting dressed himself.

"I mean, how are you feeling?" Although he's smiling, he pointedly looks toward my arms, indicating my insatiable need for the dirty drug.

I pause tying my shoelaces and rub my lips together as I think about his question. "I'll be fine," I finally reply. Ben scoffs and shakes his head. "What?"

"You don't have to be so hard all the time. I just want to make sure you're okay. What you've been through has been—"

"I've been through so much," I cut him off. "What do you want me to say? I crave it? Well, I do. But I'll be fine. I'm stronger than you think."

"You don't have to convince me of that. You're incredible. There's really no other way to describe you, but *incredible.* I'm in total awe of you."

I hold my hand up to stop Ben. "I..." My phone ringing interrupts us. "Yeah," I answer.

"Get out now," Agent says. "Fucking facial recognition has identified Ben close to the hotel. The police are contacting security at every hotel in the area to check their cameras."

"How long do we have?" I finish tying my shoelace and jump to my feet. Ben stares at me, waiting for my response.

"Maybe twenty minutes."

"Get Doctor back here now."

"Already done, he's on his way."

I place the earpiece in just as Doctor enters the room. "You both need to move."

I point to my earpiece. "Get us directions out of here," I say to Agent.

"I'm already working on that."

"Have you made the call about the brothel yet?"

"Not yet. I have forty-two minutes before I make the call."

"Get a record of all the girls who are rescued, and give their names and addresses of their families to Doctor."

"On it. You need to move."

I look to Doctor and the pile of cash on the bed. "Here." I take two wads and throw it at Ben. "Divide the cash and give it to the girls. They're going to need all the help they can get to detox." Doctor nods and stands aside from the door. "Get a different hotel for Doctor right now. I don't want him caught up in this," I instruct Agent.

"On it."

I turn to Doctor and say, "Agent will call you with instructions."

"15, they're out on the street," Agent says.

"Fuck," I look to Ben. "Create a diversion." This is what sparks me to the edge of excitement. On the verge of being caught, but being just that one tiny step ahead. My heart pumps and my skin tingles with ecstasy.

"Wait, don't go out yet. Give me five seconds," Agent says.

"Empty the trash liner and use it to carry the money." Ben overturns the trash and rips out the liner, then stuffs the cash into it and hands it to Doctor. Suddenly, the hotel's alarms sound, followed by another alarm, then another.

"There are four hotels on the same block, and all of the fire alarms are going off at the same time. Wait until I give you the go-ahead to leave the room."

I'm at the door first, waiting for Agent's signal. Ben has my hand gripped in his, and Doctor is waiting behind us with the plastic bag and his fedora. "Doctor, you go out first. Ben and I will follow."

"Go," Agent says.

"Go." I open the door and wait for Doctor to slip out first, then wait another few seconds before integrating into the crowd as they all leave their rooms and head outside. There's an announcement over the hotel PA system for everyone to remain calm and to head out the front of the building.

This is a perfect cover for Ben and me to slip away, and for Doctor to make his way to the new hotel for the night.

When Ben and I get out to the street, there are police and fire trucks everywhere. People are rushing out from everywhere. The street has been closed off from one end of the block to the other, with more sirens screaming as vehicles speed toward the hotels.

"What's going on?" I hear a woman ask one of the hotel staff.

"Please make your way over to the evacuation point," the staff member says and indicates toward where the woman should go.

I glance at Ben beside me, and we mill closer to all the people. The crowd quickly grows, making it nearly impossible for us to be found. "15," Agent says through the earpiece.

"Yeah?"

"Walk east until you reach the end of the block, and turn left."

While blending in, we make our way toward the destination Agent chose for us. "Have you got us?"

"I've got you through your GPS. Follow this street until you reach Market Street on your right." Ben and I pick up our pace, still remaining cloaked under the commotion of the mass exodus. "Next right." I spot a convenience store up ahead. Thankfully it's dark, but we still need to remain incognito. "When you take that street, continue down to the harbor. It's about a mile walk."

"Ben." He looks over at me. "I need some money." As we walk, he reaches into his pocket and hands me a few bills. "Stay out here."

I duck into the store and look at the trinkets they have on sale. In particular, hats, sunglasses and a couple of furry stuffed animals of kangaroos and koalas. I also grab a couple of bottles of water and take the items up to the counter. I try to keep my head down as I pay for everything. "Would you like a bag?" the attendant asks.

"Yes thanks."

"Bags are twenty cents."

"That's fine." He scans everything and places the items in the bag. I pay, then take the bag and leave. "Here," I say to Ben and take one of the caps out for him. I too wear a cap as we continue following Agent's directions.

"Are you trying to tell me something?" Agent asks. "Furry stuffed animals?"

"You're an idiot. They were bought as a decoy, so it looks like we're just sightseeing tourists." Ben looks at me and crinkles his brows. "Agent." Ben snickers. I'm finding it difficult to keep going. The abuse to my body while being force-fed drugs means I'm not as agile as I usually am or have my usual stamina. "How far to where we're supposed to be?"

"You have a good ten minutes."

"Are you okay?" Ben asks as we continue to power walk the distance.

"I'll push through."

"Once you're down at the harbor, look for a small boat on the furthest left side called the Sea Piper. The guy's waiting for you, his name is Peter."

"Payment?" I ask.

"Taken care of," Agent replies. "He'll get you to a cargo ship that's already left the dock. They're waiting for you."

"Have you got visual on Doctor?"

"He's en route to the other hotel."

"Get him out of the country safely, Agent."

"He's flying back home first class, unlike you." Agent snickers.

"I've also org—" The line goes dead. I take the cell out of my pocket and look at the screen. It's blank. I try turning it back on, but the battery icon appears on the screen telling me the phone is completely dead.

"Shit," I say. "Ben, check your phone. How much charge have you got?"

He looks to his phone and turns it so I can see how much charge he has. "Not much."

"Power it down, because we don't know when we're going to need it." I'm such an idiot. I should've bought a portable charger back at the convenience store. I blame the effects of the drugs and me still detoxing from them.

Within moments, we're walking past the nightlife of fancy restaurants on the water's edge of Darling Harbour. "It's so quiet," Ben says.

"It is after midnight."

"Yeah, but I thought it would be busier than what it is."

"We're looking for a boat called the Sea Piper, and the captain's name is Peter," I say as we head toward all the boats.

It doesn't take Ben long to find it. "Here," he says and takes the lead toward the boat.

Jesus, that's a fucking boat? It's small and looks like it's held together with duct tape. The writing on the side is faded and the boat itself looks more like a tugboat than an actual boat. We get to it and there's a man, possibly in his midthirties, sitting on a piling near where the boat is anchored. He's eating a burger while sipping on a beer. "Peter?" I ask as I stand taller.

I need to rest. My body is protesting, and I'm on the edge of collapse.

He looks me up and down, then moves his gaze to Ben. A deep frown furrows his brows as he squints at us. He takes another bite of his burger, then huffs. "15," he says as he looks to Ben. Ben glances at me. "A chick. Cool." He shoves the last of the burger in his mouth, grabs his beer, and stands. "Come on, then," he says between chews.

"You okay?" Ben whispers.

"I need sleep."

Ben gets into the tugboat, then holds his hand out to help me in. Peter unhooks the boat from the wharf and heads over to the controls. "We'll be intercepting the cargo carrier in approximately three hours, so sit back and relax." He starts the boat and slowly navigates the water.

Within moments, the boat is already heading out. I open the bag and take out a bottle of water. I take a long drink, then screw the lid back on. "Fuck," Ben groans as he places his hand to his stomach.

"Do you get seasick?" I ask with humor.

"No." His pale face indicates that he's lying.

"Once we make our way out of the Harbour, you'll find it the rockiest part of the trip. It's because it's where the warm water meets the cold which makes the boat rock quite badly. Hope you two are good on rough seas."

"I'm fine," I say.

"So am I." Ben quickly spins and vomits over the side of the boat.

"Yeah, mate, it's gonna get worse."

"Fucking great," Ben curses.

I can't help but laugh. This has got to suck for him. For me, I find it amusing. Oh well, he'll get over it. "I'm gonna close my eyes for a bit," I say as I wrap my arms around my body and close my eyes.

The sound of Ben heaving should have me worried, but he's fine. It's just motion sickness.

CHAPTER ELEVEN

ANNA

"Hey, we're here," Ben rouses me from sleep. "You were out of it. Not sure how you could sleep through that."

The tugboat is quite unsteady as it maneuvers beside the cargo boat. Neither have stopped, so we have to do this in motion.

Thankfully, it's pitch black out here and no one can see us. But that also makes maneuvering the ladder overhead quite tricky.

"You okay?" I ask Ben.

"Seen better days," he replies as he puffs his cheeks out.

"You'll be better once you're on the cargo ship," Peter announces.

"Everything went okay?" I ask Peter.

"She'll be right, mate." What? Who is *she*? Are we meeting with someone?

"Huh?" Ben asks.

"Yeah, no worries," he says.

"What?" I ask.

Peter laughs. "Bloody Yanks, taking everything so literally."

Ben waves his hand at Peter. "I have no idea what you're talking about. And, I'm too seasick to worry."

"Everything went well," Peter says.

"If you just said that to start with, then we'd already be on the damn ship." Ben shakes his head. He grabs the rope ladder and tugs on it. "Okay, you go first and then I'll be right behind you," he says to me.

"Okay." I turn to Peter and give him my thanks with a sharp nod. Climbing up the ladder is shit. It's cold and windy and dark, and one misstep will ensure I'm overboard and gone forever. I'm careful as I climb up, and when I finally reach the top, I'm greeted by the captain.

"15," he says as he holds his hand out to me. "I'm Captain Garcia. Welcome aboard."

I take his hand to shake, and I'm surprised that I don't get that deadly feeling. Either that, or the drugs have fucked up my senses. I hope not, because that could lead me into some predicaments I don't want to be in. "Do you have some place for us?"

"Yes, of course."

I turn to look down the side of the cargo ship and can only just make out Ben coming up the rope ladder. He reaches the top and I hold my hand out for him. He grabs it, and I hoist him up while he lunges forward. The tugboat pulls away from the cargo ship and quickly disappears into the night. "Everything okay?"

"Yeah, I'm glad we're off that fucking blow-up mattress," Ben replies.

He really doesn't do well with seasickness. "This way, 15," the captain says as he leads the way. "I'm sure you understand you can't be seen by any of my crew."

"We understand," I say as we quickly follow behind him.

He leads us through a maze of containers, then climbs a set of stairs. He comes to a shipping container that's unhooked and slightly ajar. The door swings open a little, then closes again. "Here you go." He opens the container further. "You'll need these." He removes two small torches from his pockets. He flicks one on, and shines it inside. "There's two more torches there." He points the light on the inside of the container. "You can unlock it from the inside, here." He quickly shows us how to unlock the container.

"Thank you," Ben says as he takes the torch he's holding.

The captain gives us a curt nod and leaves. Inside the container there's a bed with blankets, some canned food, a camping toilet, and small portable sink. I have no idea if it has running water, but who cares? This is a means to an end, and if it means I can get back to America, I'll be compliant and take what I can get.

"I need to talk to Agent, but I can't use the little battery you have left on your phone. Besides, we're in the middle of the ocean."

"Let's rest for now, and we'll talk to the captain tomorrow. That fucking boat ride has taken it out of me, Anna." I shouldn't but... I burst into laughter. Ben tackles me to the bed where we stay entwined in one another. "Are you laughing at me?"

"I'm not laughing at myself."

"The waters were rough, okay." He kisses my forehead.

"If you say so. I slept through it."

"You're a freak of nature. Is there anything that makes your skin crawl? Snakes, spiders, clowns?"

"Clowns?" I look up at him and shake my head.

"You have to have a flaw. You can't be perfect all of the time."

"Perfect?" I lift my brows and wrestle out of his tight hug. "There's not one single thing about me that's perfect. Other than I'm good at killing."

Ben lies back on the bed, looking up at the inside of the container as I take my shoes off and sit cross-legged, watching him. "That's where you're wrong. You are the perfect female, and I'm damn lucky you're mine."

I smack his leg making him turn to look at me. "I'm yours?" I ask with a tilt of my head.

"Obviously," he says seriously. "Like I'm yours."

I crinkle my brows, somehow surprised by his admission. "I've been on my own for so long, that..."

"Well, you're not alone now," he says. "Now, we're together." He closes his eyes and exhales loudly. I guess we've kind of already had this conversation in the past. "I'm tired, and I want to go to sleep." I stay staring at him for a moment longer. "I hate ships," he finally admits.

I smile as I lie beside him and close my eyes. Ben is snoring within moments of closing his eyes, while I stay awake, wondering how different my life would've been if I just killed Ben an eternity ago.

Finally, the exhaustion of the day, the drugs still lingering in my body, and the excitement of killing sends me to sleep.

I open my eyes and feel the urgent need to go to the bathroom. I look beside me to find the bed empty. Pushing the covers back, I notice the door to the shipping container is open. It swings open and closed as we travel on the water. "Hey," Ben says as he walks into the container.

"Can you go out?" I flick my hand at him.

"Why?"

"I need to pee."

He chuckles but nods and heads out. Once finished, I wash my hands with the slow, thin stream of water delivered by the sink. If they can get water to a faucet, then why couldn't they have a flushing toilet? I remind myself to appreciate what I have.

I open the door and find Ben standing nearby. "Done?"

"Yeah. Where were you?"

Ben lowers his chin as his shoulders hunch forward. "I had to vomit. I thought it would be best if I do it over the edge of the ship." *Contain the laughter, Anna.* "Looking down on the water from so high is fucking scary." *Stop talking or I'm going to laugh.* "I could never have joined the navy." *Please shut up.* "I think my DNA is down half the cargo ship."

That's it, I can't help it. The laugh I've been stifling finally releases. "You're so cute," I say.

He lifts his chin and attempts to silence me with a deadly look. "Stop it," he snaps. "I need to rinse my mouth out." Ben enters the container and I follow behind, still laughing. He grabs a bottle of water from the supplies provided for us, rinses his mouth, and spits it down the sink. "Remind me to never go on a cruise ship."

"Let's hope Agent hasn't booked us on one."

Ben rolls his head back and groans. "Ugh, I need Doctor," he complains comically.

"Sorry, Doctor looks after me. Get your own Doctor."

"You won't share?" He looks at me with a slight chin quiver and big puppy dog eyes.

"At least you're entertaining," I call over my shoulder as I look for something to eat. There's an array of canned goods, and I open a can of mixed fruit and eat half before having some water.

"How are you feeling? Any withdrawals?"

"If I think about it, then all I want to do is tear through the ship and find some. But, I'm trying not to think about it." Except he just reminded me of it.

I slow my chewing as that ever-so-familiar snake-bite feeling begins to slide through me. Cold washes over every inch of my skin, and I look outside waiting for something to happen. Something isn't right; it makes the hair on the back of my neck stand to attention.

Ships like this can often be attacked by pirates wanting to steal whatever treasures may be on board. "Get your phone out, call Agent," I instruct as I quickly put my shoes on and get ready for a quick escape. Although, we're in the middle of the ocean. Fuck, I hope the phone works.

"It's not working."

"Give it a second, Agent will somehow connect to us." Ben eagerly tries to find service through the phone. And, just like I knew, the phone rings. "Agent," I say as I snatch the phone out of Ben's hand.

The calm sea does nothing to relax my unease. I *know* something is off. "There's an incoming helicopter."

I look around, unable to see anything. "What's the ETA?" I try to make this fast, because my phone is dead, and Ben's battery is nearly gone too.

"Six minutes."

"You need to get on that—" The phone dies.

"Fuck," I try rebooting the phone, but the red battery symbol appears, telling me I need to charge the phone. "A helicopter will be landing within minutes, and we need to be on it."

Ben looks around, then runs over to the stairs and climbs to the top. "Up here." He points toward a deck where the helicopter has space to land.

As we near the landing pad, the sound of the rotors becomes louder and louder. "Move," I yell to Ben so we're there by the time the helicopter lands.

There's a part of me that's still dealing with the detox, but I push that part down because we need to make it off this cargo ship. We reach the landing pad just as the helicopter appears and begins to descend. The ship is still gliding through the seas toward its destination.

I keep a careful eye on our surroundings in case we're ambushed. The snake-bite feeling intensifies. Something is off, but I can't see anything at the moment.

The helicopter lowers and without turning the engine off, the door opens. Ben and I duck and run toward it. We enter, and there are two men in the front. An old man with thick, gray hair and beside him is the pilot.

The old man touches his headset and points to the two hanging in the back as he looks at me and taps his headset again. I put on the headset, as does Ben. I glance at Ben, then quickly scan the interior for any weapon I can get my hands on. What's going on here?

"I'm not going to hurt you," the old man says in a thick accent. Is it Russian, Belarusian, Ukrainian? Maybe a mixture of all. I really have no idea.

"Take off in five, four, three..." the pilot counts down and when he reaches one, the helicopter rises and begins our journey.

I haven't used this pilot before. "How did you land this on a moving ship?" I ask.

He looks over his shoulder and runs his gaze over my body. "Because I'm good at what I do," he replies arrogantly. His cocky reply causes me to smirk. I like him; I think I'll add him to my payroll.

"Where are we going?" I'm hoping he has the next destination from Agent. "Can I charge my phone?" I look around for a power outlet.

"Why in such a hurry, Anna Brookes?" the old guy asks.

Anna Brookes? What the fuck is going on? Who is this man? How does he know who I am?

Panic bubbles inside my gut, and I know I need to kill this fucker right now. "Who are you?" I automatically become defensive. There's nothing back here I can kill him with. I'll have to do it the old-fashioned way, with my hands.

"I'm a friend, and I'm here to help you find an enemy. One who has wronged you and who does not know who you are."

"Vang," I whisper as I glance at Ben.

Ben gestures with his eyes toward the old man and slightly lifts his shoulders. He doesn't know who the old man is either.

"Yes, Vang," the old man confirms.

"Who are you?" I pull my shoulders back, ready to take this entire helicopter down if I don't get my answer.

"I'm a friend," he repeats. "Vang is hiding, and I will...how you say it? доставить его на блюдечке с голубой каемочкой." He chuckles at his own words. The old man is Russian, his dialect thick and punchy. He turns to look at me, and quickly assesses my unamused tone. "I say, I will deliver him to you on silver platter." He laughs again. Although his English is nearly intelligible, it's still encapsulated within his accent.

"Why? What do you want in return?" Nothing is ever given for free. There's always an exchange of some sort. Usually it's money, but in this case, I suspect he wants something else. *Power.*

Ben places his hand on my thigh and gently squeezes to grab my attention. I look over at him, and he slightly shakes his head. He wants me to calm and listen before I wrap my fingers around the old man's throat and squeeze whatever life he has left out of him.

"I want nothing. I want you to know where he hides."

"Why? Inherently there's an exchange of some value. What do you want?" There's no use in dancing around this. "You want something. What is it?"

"I help you because you're important."

I feel like this is a trick statement. Obviously, I'm essential. I rid the world of dangerous human vermin. "Why am I important?" The curiosity has gotten the better of me.

"Because, my dear, you are *very* important to me."

Is that it? I'm important to him? Why? "I'm not going to work for you."

He throws his head back and laughs. "I no want you to work for me." He waggles his finger at me.

I have no idea what's going on. Who is this man? How did Agent find him? Is Agent in on this? What the fuck is going on? "Then why am I important to you?"

The old man chuckles once again and turns in his seat to stare at me. "You and your sister matter greatly to me."

My fucking what?

I've got a sister? Where did she come from? How is she my sister?

My mouth falls open as I drop my chin and furrow my brows trying to make sense of what this old man has said. My hands shake as I run through every memory I have. I'm an only child, I don't have...

Wait, what if my mother, Natalia, had another child after me? Before me?

I know I'm Dad's only daughter, what if he...?

What am I thinking?

"I have a sister?" I ask in a small, disbelieving voice. "I can't."

"*Da*, you do," the old man confirms. "She is very beautiful, like you."

"Who is she?" I ask, suddenly consumed by the fact I have a sister. No, he's lying, I can't have a sister. But what if I do? "Who is she?" My hands clench and I'm ready to tear through the helicopter to find out the truth. "Who are you?"

"I am friend. A good one."

"I don't believe you," I spit as I attempt to calm my mind.

"You will meet. Soon. But for now, we take you to the Philippines, where you will find who you are searching for. I have organized for you to have all the supplies you need. You have your own man, *da*?" I stare at him blankly. I'm not giving this fucker anything. "The man you call Agent." How the fuck does he know this? "He is a good man, *nyet*?"

I purse my lips together and stare at him coldly. "What do you want?" I ask without giving him an answer. Although judging by what he's told me, he already knows the answers.

There's a condescending smirk on his face. "You must be hungry." He reaches into a freezer bag beside him and holds out a bottle of water for me to take. I eye it suspiciously and look away. "You think I drug you?" he asks with an obvious pang of hurt to his tone.

"I don't know you," I reply.

He unscrews the bottle's lid, and brings it to his lips, taking a sip before replacing it. He then holds it out. Ben takes it and shakes his head at me. "You don't drink from it until I know it's safe." He unscrews the lid and drinks from the bottle. Lowering it, we both wait a moment, but nothing happens. "Here." Ben gives me the bottle and I guzzle it.

"Here." The old man holds a second bottle of water, but it's unopened.

"Don't take it," I say to Ben who's reaching his hand out.

The old man huffs, and repeats the process before Ben takes it and drinks some. "Here." The old man produces a sandwich from the same bag. He unwraps it, opens it and shows the filling. Chicken and mustard. He takes a bite, chews and swallows it before handing it over to us. He repeats it with a second sandwich. "Good?" Ben and I welcome the food, although I'm still skeptical. "After you kill Vang, I take you back to America."

I stare at the old man. I don't know what it is, but he's somehow familiar to me. I can't even explain what it is, and it goes against every fiber of my being to trust him, but for some stupid reason, I do. "What do you know about Vang?"

"He is in hiding from what your Agent brought on him. The Yakuza believe he deceived them and they also think he is hiding in the province of Mindanao."

Ben looks to me and his brows knit together. He opens his mouth to say something, but stops before he lets anything slip out. He purses his lips together and looks down to the floor of the helicopter. "Mindanao? Are you positive?"

"*Da*, I'm sure. Why you question me?" the old man snaps. His jaw twitches and he rubs his hand across the back of his neck. He's irritated with Ben's inquiry.

"I'm surprised, because if he was hiding in Mindanao, the militants would've captured and tortured him by now. They don't take kindly to the Japanese since the occupation back between forty-two and forty-five. The Japanese were cruel and inhumane to the Filipinos, so now they hate them with passion."

In disbelief, I stare at Ben. He sounds like a walking Google-fact. How the hell does he know that? Even I don't. And, I'm smart. Note to self: ask Ben about his knowledge of this once Katsuo has been dealt with.

"*Da*, you are right. He isn't hiding in Mindanao, but I make sure Yakuza believe he is. He's in province of Millspot, in a village called Starshade, hiding in a hut near the mountains."

"How do you know this?" I hope his information is good and I won't be walking Ben and myself into a trap.

"I made sure to lead him where you want him, *da*? He expects Yakuza to find him, and he is about to move. He no expect you."

I look out the window and stare at the blue ribbons of sea beneath us. We're flying low across the ocean. The low altitude must be so we remain undetected. The sea goes on for what feels like forever with no sign of land nearby.

The thought of killing Katsuo is trumped by the discovery that I have a sister. I don't know who she is, how old she is, or even where she's been all my life. Why did Natalia never tell me about my sister? Wait, is she Lincoln Murphy's? No, she can't be, he would've boasted about her like he did about my mother. "Tell me about my sister," I say into the headphones.

The old man glances to the pilot, then ahead. He sits back in the seat and takes a breath. He can't drop something so monumental on me and not say anything about her. "Your sister..." he starts but quickly stops, taking in another dramatic breath. "She is different, she's nothing like you."

I don't know if I should be relieved or upset. "What do you mean?" I absentmindedly link my fingers with Ben's. He squeezes gently and when I look over to him, he offers me a small nod.

My throat dries as I wait for the old man to grant me some kind of information about her. *Anything*. "She does things her way."

"What does that even mean? How old is she? What does she do?" I need to protect her. I have to make sure she's nothing like me, and no one can ever go after her.

"You'll see soon enough," the old man replies cryptically.

This is one of the few times in my life that I don't know what's happening. As a matter of fact, my life started spiraling out of control the moment I decided not to kill Ben. But if I had, then I may never have found out that I have a sister. "Tell me about her," I say, insisting he give me something. "Her name, her age, anything," I find myself begging. Something I don't ever do. But I need to know about her.

Who is she? If she's young, I'll find the best school in the world for her. I'll make sure she has her own security entourage, who'll protect her with their lives. If she's older, I'll buy whatever she's interested in so she can run it. If she's into fashion, I'll send her to the best fashion schools in the world, then set up whatever business she wants. If it's music she's into, then I'll find her the best vocal coach and get her an agent to represent her. I don't care what it costs; I don't care about any of it. All I want is for her not to be like me.

She has to have a heart and a soul. I can't ever let her know who I am or what I do.

She's way too important to be tainted by darkness.

"Sleep now, for soon we'll arrive at Millspot."

I don't want to sleep, but my body is still fighting the niggling pull of the drugs. Not to mention the fixation I have on the knowledge of having a sister.

I have a sister.

Wringing my hands together I feel my body quaking with an emotion I only experience when I'm on the hunt to kill. Excitement fills me. I'm not entirely sure I can sleep with this newfound information.

I can't wait to finally meet her.

But, what if she doesn't want to meet me?

Wait, is meeting her really a good idea?

I look out over the vast seas and consider my options. I don't know what to do.

Chapter Twelve

Anna

True to his word, the old man left us at Millspot, with supplies and no further answers about my sister.

He also didn't tell me who he was, but he gave us a number to call when Ben and I want to return to the States.

I have Agent for that.

I touch my earpiece and connect with Agent. "15," he answers.

"When will my supplies be here?"

"I'm amazed you're awake considering you landed only a few hours ago." I don't reply to his ridiculousness. "Right then," he says with tension. "You'll have your supplies coming in three hours and forty-two minutes."

There are a lot of questions I have for Agent, but for now, I need to get to Katsuo. I'll deal with Agent when I return to home soil. "The pedophiles?"

"I have their locations."

"Good." I nod once and look out of our bungalow.

There's a tense pause between us. "Do you need anything else?"

I grind my teeth together as I stop myself from asking questions now. I tap my earpiece and hang up. I take it out of my ear and drop it on the bed as I head out to find Ben. The huts are small, yet cozy. The humidity is quite high, causing my tank top to stick to my skin. I leave the small hut and walk toward the center of town. It's not even a town, more like a paved road filled with vendors selling food on either side. It's not congested with tourists, but there are a few. The ones who'd rather be among the locals than fall into the tourist traps.

"Hey," I say to Ben as he picks up some local delicacies for us. I place my hand to his hot and sweaty back.

He startles beneath my touch. "Hey," he says and leans down to give me a kiss on the mouth. "I was going to bring you back some food." He holds up paper bags. "Did you sleep okay?"

"Yeah, I called Agent. Supplies will be here in a few hours."

Ben holds out some money to one of the vendors in exchange for fresh fruit. "Here." He hands me two massive mangoes. The sweet aroma coming from them is divine and makes me want to tear into them. We begin the short walk back to the hut as Ben unscrews a water bottle and takes a sip. "He was easy to track down."

"You found Katsuo?" I ask with surprise.

"I left you asleep and went exploring. He's about fifteen minutes east."

"Did he see you?"

Ben shakes his head. "I was careful, even though he isn't."

I click my tongue and let out a small sigh. "He's not being careful?"

"Nope. He was out for an early morning stroll, taking his time."

"What a fool."

"Perhaps he thinks he's safe out here. It's quite off the beaten track, and it's not like there are a lot of tourists."

"Which is why he should have been more careful. Regardless, he has to die, and he's going to, tonight."

We return to our hut, and Ben lays out the food he's bought. All of it is local food, and nothing I've ever had before. I stick to the foods that appear simple, without a lot of heat and spice. I'd hate to be sick when I torture Katsuo. "Do you wonder if Vang thinks about you?" Ben asks as he sits back on the chair and eats.

"I couldn't care less whether he thinks about me or not. But I know he'll be regretting selling me into the sex trade while I'm torturing him." Ben smirks as he shoves more food into his mouth. "We'll do it tonight. I want to end him, and get out quickly."

"Are the plans in place for us to leave?"

"When we arrived and I spoke with Agent he said he's preparing our exit route. I'll know more later."

Ben lifts his foot and places it on the chair beneath him, his knee up high as he eats. "Are you okay to do this tonight?"

"That fucker sold me into the sex trade." I lower my food and place it on the small table between us. "Not only will I be okay, I'm already planning on what I want to do to him."

"I take it this isn't going to be a quick death?"

"Your intuition is right. I'm going to hurt him, and I'm going to make sure he knows who I am."

"Want to let me in on the fun you're going to have?" He looks across at me as he eats his food, a small smirk tugging at his lips.

"Maybe later." I smile and wink. "But he's not going to like it."

"I have no doubt you'll bring the pain. Should I see if I can round up some rats?"

I flick my hand and roll my eyes. "Rats are *so* last season."

"Good Lord," Ben grumbles. He leans over and pushes the sliced mango toward me. "Try that. It's so good."

I eat a slice of mango as I think about what I want to do to Vang. He's going to suffer, and I'm going to love every moment of it. "Yeah, I like this." Ben stares at me as I inhale the mango. "What?"

"Do you know you have beautiful eyes?" My unimpressed scowl makes Ben laugh. "I'm paying you a compliment, Anna. That's all."

"You don't need to romance me. I'm not the type of woman who needs that."

"I'm just saying, our kids will have pretty eyes."

For the first time in my life, I'm speechless. It takes what feels like hours before I actually reply. "Kids?" Ben nods. "I'm not maternal. I don't want them."

"Maybe one day that might change."

"If kids are something you really want, then I suggest you leave now. Because I can't bring a child into my world. I'm not cut out for that. I never have been."

"But…"

"Ben, it's not in my future." Ben lowers his chin as he slices through another mango. "If that's something you want, I'm not the person for you."

He shakes his head and pulls his shoulders back. "It was just a thought. Nothing more." He slides another slice of mango over toward me. I pick it up and eat it, but now I feel like an ass for crushing Ben's dreams of us being a happy family.

Happy families and assassins don't mix.

Ever.

Agent is brilliant. He sent everything I need for what I have planned for Katsuo.

I double-check the inventory lying on the bed while I go over the plan again in my head. Ben is dressed in his blacks, like me, and I'm pulling my hair back into a severe ponytail as I carefully assess my tools of fun—or torture—on the bed.

"Do you need anything?" Ben asks.

"Give me a minute," I say as I lift each item and triple-check it.

Everything is perfect, and I can't wait to have my fun with Katsuo. My heart is racing, but not from nervousness; it's racing from the sheer elation that I'm doing what I'm good at, to someone who so richly deserves it. This is personal. This is a hit to live—for me, not for him.

There's an intoxicating drumming in my chest. My body is wired and buzzing. This is what I do. I kill people.

The energy running through me keeps me hyperaware of every single sound around me. I want this, I *crave* this. Killing is my drug, not heroin. It runs deep in my veins, desperately clawing at me for another taste. I lick my lips and smirk as I mentally prepare for the immense fun I'm about to have.

I can't wait to see the sheer terror on his face when he sees me. When he realizes his breaths are numbered.

I lift the duffel onto the bed, and meticulously ensure everything is in the bag. Katsuo will die tonight, by my hand alone. And I'm going to fucking love it.

I zip the bag and Ben lifts it off the bed and heads toward the door. I sit on the edge of the bed and close my eyes. I'm in the zone, but I need to calm my excitement down. I have a job to do, and I don't want to get sloppy and make a mistake.

I calm my breathing, and begin my ritual. Centering myself while I become completely and utterly in tune with myself and my sur-roundings.

The familiar wave of clarity is welcome, and the deep desire to kill hums through my body along with the excitement.

I hear the scurry of small feet outside the window, possibly a native animal. Ben's breathing as he stands, waiting for me. I can feel his heat even though I know he's a few feet from me. A bird makes a light sound. Perhaps it's calling for its mate, or maybe it's about to strike its prey.

I snap my eyes open as a blanket of ice causes my skin to pebble with anticipation. Katsuo has caused too much devastation to live, and for that, he'll die. *Now.*

Pushing up from the bed, I walk over to Ben and grab his shirt. Dragging him down, I hungrily kiss him. I find myself smiling, remembering the last time I did this. When we were on our way to the brothel to end the lives of those who bought me and had profited off the lives of many innocent women and girls.

I release Ben and step backward. "You ready?" he asks as he squats to take the duffel. The left part of my lip lifts higher than the right as I arch a brow. "I take it by that look your answer is yes."

"Hell, yes."

"Let's go."

Ben and I fall into our own routine. He's my muscle, and I'm the killer. My favorite pleasure in life is to watch someone die who deserves it. To watch as they struggle to breathe, panic filling their eyes until they finally take their last breath.

My absolute fucking pleasure.

We walk through the small community without notice, Ben carrying the duffel with all my toys. The walk to where Katsuo is staying takes no more than fifteen minutes. I'm completely in the zone, prepared for one of my best kills.

Covered by an inky sky and peaceful surroundings, I'm reminded of the mission I'm on. The people of these towns need protecting from men like Katsuo, even if they don't know it yet. I'm here for them, for me, and for Ben's sister Claire. After tonight, Vang will never harm another person.

We reach the small community where Katsuo is staying and stop a mere hundred feet from his hut. "Remember the plan," I whisper to Ben.

"I've got it." He touches his earpiece and whispers, "Testing."

"You're good."

With nothing more than a slight smile and nimble steps, Ben disappears into the darkness. I quickly head toward the hut and duck behind a spray of shrubs. A snake passes between my legs and slithers into the forest. "In place," he whispers. "Going in five, four, three, two..."

I need only wait for a few seconds before I hear the door being kicked in. Within milliseconds, the other door opens and Katsuo runs out while looking over his shoulder. He turns back and comes face-to-face with me. Katsuo abruptly stops, his eyes wide with fear, and as an added bonus for me, his chin has a tiny quiver of distress.

"Katsuo," I greet him as I jab a syringe filled with a paralytic agent into his neck. He tries to run but the drug takes instant effect, and he collapses at my feet. Ben is right there to pick him up and carry him inside.

I close the door as best I can, then turn to keep staring at Katsuo. Ben releases him and Katsuo slumps to the floor, while I squat beside him. "That needle contained a drug to paralyze your muscles, which means you can't stop anything I'm going to do to you, nor can you try to get away."

"Kitchen table?" Ben asks.

"It's the perfect height for me to work."

Ben clears the table, making sure not to make too much noise, because the small community is quiet at this late hour of the night. "Will this do?" Ben holds up a beaten up stockpot.

"Perfect."

Ben picks Katsuo up and places him on the table. Beads of sweat form across his forehead and his eyes furiously move back and forth. "You're fucked." Ben snorts as he looks to Katsuo. Ben pats Katsuo on the head and adds, "I don't envy you, that's for sure."

"Before the drug wears off, there are a few things I need to do. First, I'm going to cut out your tongue. Then I'll be setting up two IVs. Now, while you're paralyzed, it won't hurt, because essentially the drug I gave you is also a nerve blocker. Rest assured, I do have plans for other things that will hurt. But I can't have you screaming and drawing attention to us." Ben stands back and watches as I talk to Katsuo. "You might pass out because of the pain when the blockers wear off, but don't worry, I'll wait until you come around before I continue with the pain."

"When do you want me to record this?" Ben asks as he lifts his phone from his pocket.

"Start now."

Ben sets the phone up on a tripod on a nearby shelf, and begins to record us. "Hmmm." I tap my finger to my mouth. "I'm going to do

something spontaneous, Katsuo. I won't cut your tongue out, yet."
Ben has quickly laid out everything on the counter behind the table.
"First, I'll insert two IVs. One of them will extract the blood from
your body, the other will put it back in. I'll be adding solvent to the
returning blood. Do you want to know what this is going to do to
you?" I gently run my hand down Katsuo's cheek. "You'll feel like
your body is on fire while the solvent attacks your organs, shutting
them down at a slow, yet painful pace."

A tear slowly rolls from the corner of his eye. "Is he crying?" Ben
asks in a mocking, heartless voice.

"Yep," I confirm. I place a torniquet around his upper arm and
smack his forearm so a vein pops, then jab the needle into his arm.
"Ouch, that would've hurt." I look over to Katsuo and lift my shoulders. "Maybe I didn't get it right, let me try again." I purposely poke
more holes into him before finally getting the first IV set up. The
blood starts dripping down into the stockpot. "Did you know that
when a person donates blood no more than about sixteen ounces can
be taken, Katsuo? It takes up to forty-eight hours for the blood to
rejuvenate."

"Really?" Ben asks.

"Yeah." I nod up to him. "But in your case, Katsuo, I'm taking it
out, adding the solvent, and putting it straight back in." I reach across
to the bench for the solvent. I take the eyedropper's lid off and begin
to add drops into the blood pooling in the stockpot. "Now, I don't
want to add too much because that'll kill you quickly, and I need you
to suffer."

A small, deep groan escapes from Katsuo. "Oomph." Ben inhales a sharp breath and cringes.

"Let's get the second IV in and when there's enough blood, we'll let it flow back into your body."

"What do you need?" Ben asks.

"Gloves. Because the next part is going to get messy."

"You're so calm."

Sliding the first glove on, I look over to Ben and wink. "This is fun for me." Once both gloves are on, I take the scalpel and vice grips from all the instruments set up and walk to Katsuo's head. "I need your tongue." I force his jaw open, then take the vice grips and hold his tongue out. I latch the grips onto his tongue and extend it until I feel definite resistance. I slice through his tongue, but seeing as it's quite a dense muscle, I decide to leave it still attached, but only by a few strands of tissue. "The pain will be sickening when the paralyzing agent wears off." Blood flows freely down Katsuo's chin.

Ben snickers as he continues to record me.

"Mmmm," Katsuo moans as he hyperventilates.

"Good! You're starting to come out of the paralysis. But, don't worry, the blood you're losing isn't enough to make you pass out. Besides, by the time that could happen, I'll have pumped it back into you."

"Mmmm."

"Oh, I know." I place my hand to his cheek, then grab his dangling tongue and yank on it, seeing if the tissue finally releases. Alas, it doesn't. "It hurts, right?"

"Mmmm." His pinky moves and now I'm about to ramp it all up.

"I'm sorry, Katsuo, I forgot to properly introduce myself. How silly of me," I say with utmost satire. "You have no idea who I actually am."

"Mmmm."

"So rude of me." I tilt my head to stare into Katsuo's eyes. I want to see the fear and terror roll through him when he realizes who I am. "I should shake your hand, but you're paralyzed, so I'm just going to tell you my name is..." I pause, loving the sheer panic consuming Katsuo. "15."

There's a moment of absolute silence. His frantic breathing eases, his eyes soften as more tears fall from them. "Mmmm."

"Usually, I would've killed you quickly, but you sold me into the sex trade, and you addicted me to heroin. So for that, you will die slowly."

His hand loosely balls into a fist. Ben steps forward and uses the rope to tie Katsuo to the table, securing his arms and legs, so he's spread-eagled. "Grrr mmmm."

"I'm sick of your voice." I take the roll of silver duct tape and place it over his mouth. His tongue dangles beneath, I duct tape that too. "Now you've started to feel again, I'm going to make you experience every bit of pain you've ever inflicted on every girl you've hurt." I lower my head and whisper, "For every single girl you've sold into the sex trade, every girl you've allowed a pedophile to touch, for every dollar you've made off them."

I straighten my back and keep a careful eye on Katsuo.

"Right. Now you know that I'm going to hurt you. So let's start with the bleach."

"It's on the counter," Ben says.

I take the bottle of bleach off the counter and pour some into the lid. I turn to Katsuo and smile. "There's no question at all that this going to hurt. And leave you blind." I hold his right eye open and pour the contents into it.

Katsuo shrieks with pain. "Shit," Ben says as he grabs something soft to place over Katsuo's mouth, muffling the sound. "Are you always so controlled?"

"Absolutely, but Katsuo has also made me angry, which means I'm going to make him hurt everywhere."

Ben clicks his tongue and slightly shakes his head. "You did this to yourself, Vang."

Katsuo is trying to thrash around the table, but the fact he's still paralyzed is working in my favor. "Now, what about the other eye?"

Katsuo groans as I pour another lid full of bleach into his eye. "This is really going to hurt when the drug wears off."

Yep. This reaction is more out of fear than the actual pain. "He understands how much he's going to feel once his body has cleared the sedative," I confirm, making sure Katsuo knows the world of pain I'm bringing to him. "Imagine the pain you caused to all the girls and women you sold into the sex trade. You're now experiencing what they did. Uncomplicated, unemotional, helpless pain."

The more he blinks, the deeper the bleach travels. "Hmmm," he tries to gasp through the duct tape.

"Now, speaking of rape." We weren't, but that seems the natural progression of what I'm doing here. "Those girls and women were repeatedly raped, so I think it only fair you experience the trauma they experienced." I turn and take the scissors off the counter. "Out of curiosity, have you ever had anything jammed into your ass dry?" Katsuo manages to shake his head only slightly.

"I think that was a no." I cut Katsuo's pants and briefs away, leaving him completely exposed from the waist down. "I thought he'd be bigger," Ben says as he peers over his phone.

"This part is gonna hurt." I stare down at Katsuo's wild eyes, and I'm not sure if he's blind yet or not. I gently smack his cheek a few times. I look at the stockpot and I decide to increase the outgoing blood flow by adjusting the dial. "Now, if you know what's good for you, you'll stay incredibly still while I work." I chuckle. "It's not like you can go anywhere." My supplies are dwindling away as I take them off the counter one by one. "Just so you're aware, I've been planning for this since the first time you put your filthy fucking hands on me."

I hold up the thin catheter. "Man," Ben grumbles as he adjusts his stance.

"This is a catheter. Hospitals use them when a man has had an operation and needs to empty his bladder. But I'm going to use it for another reason."

"Oh," Ben cringes.

I take Katsuo's flaccid penis in my hand and shove the catheter in. "I'm not sure I did that right, hang on, let me try again." I know I'm inserting it properly. I just want him to hurt. I do it again and leave it.

"I've got sympathy pains going on," Ben murmurs.

Katsuo takes it without screaming. Impressive. Because I know the paralytic will certainly be wearing off by now. "Now this part..." I shake my head as I smile. The bright colored pipe cleaners sit on the counter. "This part is my favorite." I take the pipe cleaner in my hand and twirl it between my fingers so that Katsuo can see. "What do you think I'm going to do with this?" Katsuo's eyes are attempting to focus, and in reality, he may not even know what I'm holding. "Don't worry, you'll know what I'm doing soon enough." I carefully feed the pipe cleaner up through the catheter. I shove it as far up as I can before ripping it out in one fluid motion. "Your dick has caused too much devastation, but not anymore." Blood and other bits are hooked on the end of the pipe cleaner. "Let's go again, that was fun." I feed the pipe cleaner back up and tear it out once again.

"Fuck me." Ben closes his eyes and turns his head, trying not to look.

Katsuo is trying to scream, but the pain he must now be feeling causes him to pass out. I stop my assault on his penis, and get the second IV working. I pour his blood into a bag, and hang it up, slightly elevated, so it runs easily into his body. Without all the medical equipment I need, I make do by stacking bowls and cups on top of each other. "I have to give it to you, you're resourceful."

"Smelling salts." Ben looks to the counter and crinkles his nose. He returns his attention to the duffel bag, and finds the salts. He hands them to me. "Here."

I uncap the lid and hold Katsuo's head up as I run the bottle under his nose. The stench is sharp and horrible, enough to wake the dead. Katsuo's eyes flicker open, and just for extra measure, I run the salts under his nose again.

He's within moments of death, but I want him to feel every single thing I do to him. His attempt to appeal to my kind side is easily dismissed. His distressed groans and slight shakes of his head mean absolutely nothing to me. "I'm showing you the same kindness you've shown every female you've sold. *The same.*"

"Hmmm," he groans from beneath the tape, halfway between living and hell.

"You can't die yet." I stare at him and wonder if I tear the tape off his mouth if it'll be enough to rip his tongue out, hopefully causing more pain. Science would say probably not, but hey, let's see. With one quick movement, I tear the tape off. I'm met with resistance when I reach his tongue, so I tug harder. Katsuo shrieks in pure pain, I can't help but smile. "Damn, did that hurt?"

Katsuo's entire body is spent and he's giving up. A few harrowing sobs escape him. He moves his mouth attempting to say something, but all he's doing is moaning.

I know he's on the brink of death, and I don't have much time to keep torturing him. I lift my knife and drive it between his ribs. "For the girls you shackled." I remove the blade, and slice across his hip. Blood is spurting out from so many wounds. "For the girls you profited from." I shove the knife in the same spot on the other side of his chest. "For the girls you killed." I stab the knife into his shoulder.

Katsuo's struggling to breathe and his chest is heaving.

I have so much more I want to do to him, but based on the amount of blood he's losing it'll only be a matter of minutes before he's dead. "I'm not going to do anything more now. Instead, I'm going to enjoy watching as you take your last agonized breath."

I stand beside the monster who beat me, sold me, and injected me with heroin.

Katsuo begins to drift. His breath is slow and labored. It's beautiful to watch as his soulless, bloodied body loses the spark of life. The man who caused destruction to so many is almost dead. One more tear rolls down his cheek as his breath turns even shorter and shallower. I lean down and whisper, "If you hadn't gone after Ben, you'd still be alive." One lonely tear falls as his eyes widen and he takes his last breaths. "You brought this upon yourself."

Katsuo's eyes flicker as he intakes one last breath.

My job here is done.

Ben stands back and stares. The air between us is thick with tension. I feel lighter. Now I know I've rid the world of the monster who was Katsuo Vang.

"I have to say, that was brutal," Ben says.

I take in a deep breath and pull my shoulders back. "If you want out, I'll understand."

"I don't want out. But I have to wonder how you're going to sleep tonight."

"Without a care in the world. I did what needed to be done."

Ben tucks his phone into his pocket as he walks over toward me. He steps into my space to hug me, but I step back and start packing all our shit up. "Are you okay?"

I stop and look over my shoulder to Ben. "Do you doubt me?"

He swallows and lifts his brows. "What I witnessed would be hard for anyone to do. The only thing I'm doing is checking in on you."

I stop packing our things up and turn to look at the brutalized, mutilated body of Katsuo Vang. "You know how I can sleep at night?" Ben slowly lifts his shoulders. "I know he can't ever hurt anyone again, that's how."

"Like you said, he brought this on himself. But I'm worried about you."

"Don't be." I turn back around to take the duffel. "This is what I've been trained to do, Ben. This is my job."

"This was personal though."

"Which is why I took my time."

Ben opens his mouth to say something but hesitates. "Let's pack up and get out of here. He'll be here for at least four days before he's discovered by the villagers."

"Unless the Yakuza find him first," I say.

Ben and I continue packing up and wiping everything down in case police are called before Cleaner has a chance to get out here.

Although, I think the Yakuza will likely set the hut on fire and be done. But I can't be too careful.

Katsuo Vang, it was a pleasure killing you.

Chapter Thirteen

Anna

"The plane is en route to you," Agent says. "The pilot have your and Ben's new identities and papers. He'll take you to Singapore, where there'll be a car waiting for you and they'll take you directly to the port where you'll board a cruise liner taking you all the way to Hawaii. When you arrive, there'll be another car waiting."

"A plane? Okay." I remember Ben's reaction to the sea and try a little misdirection.

"The cruise will take ten days, and I've booked you into a suite under the guise of it being your honeymoon."

"Honeymoon?" My reaction is immediate and intense.

"You and Ben are now happily married."

"We're married, are we?" I look to Ben and shake my head. Agent finds his plans comical.

"We're what?" Ben asks. I dismissively flick my hand at him.

"Cleaner will be arriving within the next hour to take care of the hut."

"Make sure he leaves Vang where he is, but get rid of any trace of Ben and me."

"I'll relay the message to him."

"Also, give Doctor an extra hundred thousand, and Cleaner an extra ten grand."

"Done."

"Find out what you can about this sister of mine."

"I've already began the leg work. I'll have more information for you soon."

"Who was the helicopter pilot who brought us here?"

"Our regular guy was having an operation. This guy has been his backup for years. Why? Was there a problem?"

I'm keeping my cards close to my chest as I try to piece the puzzle together. "No." I disconnect the call and turn to Ben who's stretched out on the bed of the cabin we've been using.

"What is it, wife?" My lips thin as I cock a brow at him. His chuckle dies quickly. "*Anna*," Ben corrects with a clearing of his throat.

"Something isn't sitting right with me." I plonk down on the bed beside Ben. "Maybe I'm still a little hazy from the drugs."

"After what I saw you do to Vang, I think you're back in phenomenal form." He sits up and soothingly rubs his hand on my back. "What is it?"

"I don't know, but it feels like I'm being manipulated."

"By Agent?" Ben asks.

"I doubt he'd do this. If he did, he knows what would happen to him. He's far too loyal to do something underhanded. It's more about the old man and the fact he dropped that massive bombshell of having a sister."

"I've been thinking about him too."

"What are you thinking?" I ask as I cross my legs and pick at the quick around my nail.

"He literally came out of nowhere, right?" I confirm with a nod. "And he tells you, you have a sister."

"Yep."

"And he has a thick accent."

"Uh-huh."

"Do you think he may be a relative of yours? Perhaps a grandfather, or uncle, or something like that?"

"The thought did cross my mind." I wet my lips as I concentrate on my nail. "I need to find her."

"Your sister?"

"Yeah," I say on an exhale. "Maybe she's the key to this. But..." I look up at Ben. "I won't drag her into this life. I have to protect her and make sure she's never part of this." I lift my brows and look outside the open door. "She might be a kid, and if she is, I've already decided she'll have the best education I can buy, and I won't put her life in danger."

"This life isn't for a kid. But," he quickly adds. "If there's anyone in the world who'll look after her, it's you." I turn to give him a small, tight smile. "And me. Between us, we'll care for her."

I push the thought of my sister to side and jump off the bed. "We need to move because the plane is on its way to us."

Ben pushes off the bed and slides his feet into his shoes. We link our fingers together and head toward the clearing, waiting for the private plane to arrive.

My mind is racing light years ahead, but the only thing I know for certain is that I have no idea what the future holds.

"Enjoy your honeymoon," the receptionist greets us with a wide smile as we check into the cruise liner.

From the moment we left the Philippines until now, our trip has been effortless. It's about time something went smoothly, even if it's only our transportation. And thankfully, no surprise visits from an old gray-haired men.

Because Agent's booked the most expensive suite on the cruise liner, we're personally shown to our room. We're informed that we have our own private butler, and we can order anything at any time. We're introduced to our butler, and then we're left alone.

"Wow, this is nice," Ben says as he walks around the suite.

"It's fine," I reply with an indifferent shrug.

"Don't you enjoy things like this?"

"It's a means to an end, Ben. None of this matters." I look around the bottom level and begin to head upstairs.

"You really don't care about things like this, do you?"

"Why would I? It's only money, there's always more where that came from."

"You're unbelievable."

"I'm taking that as a compliment, so thank you." I smirk as I continue making my way up to the second level. Upstairs is a massive bedroom, and a bathroom that overlooks the ocean. We're isolated enough that no one would be able to see in, and if anyone does, good luck to them. "Ben," I call.

His heavy footsteps can be heard running up the stairs. "Whoa," he says when he takes in the view. "This bathroom is quite exposed."

"Who's going to look at us? The dolphins? Sharks? The fish?"

He chuckles and wraps his arms around me from behind. "Look at that tub, Anna. I think you and I should take a bath."

"Do you know how many dead skin cells would be in that tub?"

Ben tightens his arms around me as he laughs. "I'll rinse it out before I fill it, okay?"

I turn in his arms and look up at him. "Are you trying to tell me you want to have sex with me in the tub?"

"I mean…" He averts his eyes as a cheeky smirk pulls on his lips. "If my cock happens to fall into your pussy, I wouldn't say no."

I kiss his lips and release him. "You run the water. I'm going out on the balcony. Call me when the water is ready." I turn to walk away and Ben spanks my butt sharply, causing me to hop forward. "It's like that, is it?"

He tilts his head and arches a brow.

Shaking my head, I walk toward the balcony and open the sliding door. Leaning over the side, I close my eyes and take in a deep breath.

I love the smell of the ocean. It's distinct and alluring. The sea salt mixes with the gentle breeze causing my skin to pebble. Suddenly, I catch an aroma I'm all too familiar with. A sickly-sweet scent clings to the air, inviting me to breathe it in deeper. The delicious perfume coats my nostrils, and I close my eyes and lean forward to get more of the smell into me. Small vibrations of need flow through my body. I can feel it. It's calling to me like a lullaby. "Anna," it whispers. I need it, just a small taste. Just enough to take the craving away. I float closer to where the aroma is coming from.

"What the fuck?" Ben's arms around my waist snap me out of the hypnotic high of desire. "Are you trying to kill yourself?"

"What? No, of course not." The reality is I was so caught up in the moment that I was unconsciously climbing onto the railing. "I could smell it," I admit as I head inside, Ben following, and shut the balcony sliding door. "It was like I was in a trance."

Ben secures the door and turns to envelop me in his arms. He drags me into his body, securely keeping me in place. "Your heart is beating frantically," he says as he shuffles back and places his palm to my chest. "Are you okay?"

I shake my head and nestle myself firmly in his arms. "Someone is cooking heroin and I could smell it. It was like a beacon, calling to me. My mouth was parched, like I was dying of thirst but what I wanted was a taste of what they were burning on the spoon."

"I'm not letting you out of my sight."

"I don't need you to babysit me, Ben."

"I'm keeping you safe, not babysitting you."

A heavy sigh erupts from me. I break out of Ben's arms and walk over to the stairs, where I sit on the second to last one. Running my hands through my hair, I find myself fighting this. "I'm trying hard to let you into my life."

Ben nods and approaches to sit on the step beside me. "I'm not interested in taking your independence, I just want to be part of your life, Anna."

"My life has been me and me alone since Dad died. I didn't let people in. I couldn't." I look over to him and run my hand through my hair. "But I'm trying to do that with you. But..."

"Two but's in the same sentence. Wow."

"I don't need you to look after me, Ben. I can do that by myself."

"You don't have to, though. Not now. We're in this together."

I look at his dark eyes and lift my hand to skim it down his cheek. He catches my hand and kisses my palm. "I want you to let me look after you. Even if it's behind closed doors. Let me take care of you." He kisses my palm again before linking our fingers together.

I stare at him, unable to verbalize what I'm actually thinking. It takes me a long moment before I finally admit, "I don't know how. It's always been me responsible for me, and for my team. Never the other way around."

"Let me in," he whispers. "What's the worst thing that can happen?"

"I could fall in love with you." Shit, what did I say?

"I'm already in love with you." I suck in a deep, sharp breath as I try to pull away from him. He clasps his hand firmly around mine, refusing to let me get the hell out of there. "Nope." He shakes his head. "You're not going to run. Not this time." I close my eyes and lower my chin, trying to make sense of his words. His finger lifts my chin up, but I refuse to open my eyes. "Anna, we don't have to rush anything. I'm also not going anywhere. Neither are you."

I calm my breathing and finally open my eyes. "Deep down inside, I think I already knew." I purse my lips together. "But it scares me."

"Well." He stands to his feet and holds his hand out to me. "You scare the shit out of me," he adds a chuckle. "Especially when you get in the zone and you're laser-focused on killing. That shit right there is terrifying."

I'm glad he's let go of the whole "I love you" discussion. I'm not quite ready to have that discussion. Maybe one day soon. Just not yet. He pulls me up from the step and begins walking up to the second level. "What are we doing?"

"I'm going to fuck you in that bathtub."

"Now, that sounds like fun." I lift my t-shirt over my head and drop it to the floor, then unclasp my bra and drop that too. A trail of my clothes leads from the top of the stairs to the bathroom. Ben hasn't even noticed I'm already undressing until he turns around and sees me standing there in the nude. "You promised me a fucking. You'd better deliver."

"Get in the bath," he commands.

I like it when he's bossy during sex. "Yes, sir." He strips off his clothes and slides into the bath on the other end.

"Up on all fours and turn around."

Oh, yeah, this is certainly going to be fun. I look over my shoulder at him and smile. His eyes are glued to my ass. "Like what you see?" I wiggle my butt at him.

Ben grabs my hips and slows me. "Did I tell you to sit on me? I told you to back up."

Well, this is better than I thought. "I'm sorry."

Ben leans forward and with a stroke of his tongue, licks my pussy, his nose buried in the crack of my ass. "I'm gonna fuck this," he says as he pulls back and spanks me again. "But not today." He grabs onto my hips and painfully squeezes.

"Yeah," I moan as I close my eyes.

"Does my girl like having her ass spanked?" He lifts his hand and smacks me again. Delicious pain radiates through me. "You're going to back down now, and take all of me into you without stopping."

I look over my shoulder to see Ben running his hand up and down his hard cock. With my legs straddling his, I lower onto his cock. "Oh my God," I say as I close my eyes.

The water swooshes around us, some of it sloshing over the edge of the tub onto the floor. Ben snakes his hand around to my front and plays with my clit while I ride him. Slowly at first, then faster as the tension builds inside my body. With one hand on my clit, the other takes my nipple, painfully pinching and rolling it between his fingers. "Your pussy is perfect for my cock, baby." He kisses me on the back as I steady myself on the tub and continue fucking him. "Ride me hard." He continues to pinch my nipples harder as his thumb presses harder into my clit.

"That's it," I moan.

Ben moves faster, flicking, twisting, biting. His raspy breath quickens. My own senses are being awakened with the promise of release. "I need this cunt to give me everything it can."

Ben stops playing with my nipple and gently slips a finger into my ass. He's careful at first, and the sensation startles me before I find myself full and suddenly desperate for more. I want more of him inside of me. I squeeze my pussy which causes Ben to groan his own pleasure. "I want more," I shamelessly beg. I grind against his welcome intrusion in my ass. I want it. I'm loving this. "More." I move my hand from the tub to behind and clasp my hand beneath his, holding his finger firmly in place in my ass. "Give me more."

"Such a greedy girl." He nips on my shoulder. "Move your hand," Ben's voice is low and dangerous. Fuck, he's turning me on. "Hold the tub."

I close my eyes as I enjoy this full sensation. Something about being fucked like this is raw and primal. "I need this," I whimper.

Ben's fucking is animalistic. He's using me for his pleasure, and mine. His rhythm grows faster, forcing me closer to my own release. My breath is short and sharp as desire overtakes me. "That's it, give me everything you have."

My body doesn't know—*I* don't know—what to do. My control is quickly failing me. I'm about to come, *hard*. My fingers tighten on the edge of the tub, my pussy clenches on Ben's cock. I'm fighting it, I don't want to come, I want to stay in this euphoric moment a while longer. But my body is spent. I can't hold on any more. "Oh my God," I groan as my release takes over my body.

Ben grips my hip with his one free hand, his finger still in my ass, his cock deep inside me. He thrusts up hard several times as the water splashes up the side and out of the bath. "I love your fucking pussy. Milk me. Milk everything out of me," he demands as I tighten and release, tighten and release. "That's it. Give me everything."

Finally, completely spent, we both become calm. I take in several deep breaths while Ben slowly pulls his finger out, his cock still deep inside me. "Fuck," I groan. "I think my legs are jello."

"I love your pussy, but I love you more."

I smile as I lean back against Ben. He pulls out, opens his legs, and I lie between them. I think I love him too, but I'm not ready to tell him. One day soon though.

Maybe.

Chapter Fourteen

Ben

"Mr. and Mrs. Johnson, are you enjoying your honeymoon?" the waiter asks as we're shown to our seats in one of the many restaurants on the liner.

"We are. Thank you, Austin," I answer on behalf of Anna and me.

"Can I start you with a drink?"

"Two scotches please," Anna replies. "Neat."

Austin hesitates for a few seconds before nodding and leaving. I look over the menu of what's on offer for tonight. I'm trying to read it, but I'm distracted by something I've been thinking about.

"What?" Anna's ability to read people is unprecedented. I lift my chin slightly to look at Anna, who's staring at me. "The past three days you've been unusually quiet. You're thinking about something, and now you want to talk to me about it, but you don't know how to approach the subject. So..." She purses her lips together. "What is it?"

I rub at my forehead and close my eyes. "You are amazing," I say.

"I know," she replies.

Austin approaches us and places the scotches down before taking a small step back. "Are you ready to order?"

"Not yet. Give us a few minutes," I say.

"Very well." As if Austin can sense the tension at the table, he makes a diplomatic getaway. *Smart move, buddy.*

"Do you need liquid courage, Ben?" Anna lifts her glass and drinks it one easy movement.

I reach for mine and swirl it around in the glass a few times. "The thing is," I start as I continue staring at the glass. "I've been thinking about us." I carefully lift my gaze to look at Anna.

She's sitting back on the comfortable bench seat, with her arms crossed in front of her chest. "What have you thought about?" Her jaw tightens as she continues to stare at me, apparently emotionless. It's clear from her taut shoulders, wide eyes, and the slightly tilted head that she's restraining her anger. Anna arches a brow and inhales a sharp breath. "Are you going to tell me or am I expected to be a mind reader?"

"What do you think about us..." I swoop my hand in a cutting action an inch above the table. "You know?"

"If you wanted out, that's all you had to say."

"No, that's not what I want. I want us both to step away from," I pause and check over both my shoulders to make sure no one is listening. "Step away from our current occupations," I carefully say.

Anna pulls her head back with a clearly confused grimace. "And do what?"

"Something other than what we do. *Nothing*. It doesn't matter, I'm sure we have enough money between us to last us a lifetime, maybe more."

Anna's shoulders relax and she lifts her hand to take the glass. She brings it to her lips, notices it's empty then places it back on the table. "I don't think that's on the agenda for me. If you want to leave your business, then I could always use someone."

"I was hoping that neither of us would continue in our work." Anna is ruthless. There's no doubt in my mind about it.

She sits forward and crosses her arms on the table. "Why are you suggesting this?"

"It's complicated," I reply.

"Then un-complicate it."

"A part of me doesn't want to see you doing what you do anymore."

"Are you scared for me?"

"Yes," I reply earnestly. "But also no." I intake a breath and reach across for her hands. Hesitantly, Anna uncrosses her arms and extends them toward me. "You're by far the most capable person I've ever met in my life, but the week you were away from me felt like an eternity. I'm not sure I can handle that kind of thing again. It scared the ever-living shit out of me. Then when I saw you hanging off the balcony, I…" God, why is this so hard for me to say? I release her and run my hands through my hair. "I don't want you putting yourself in danger anymore. And, if that means we both retire, then I'm okay with it."

"I'm not," she replies instantly. "I don't want to stop doing what I do."

"There's going to come a time when all the skeletons are going to come at you full force."

"Yep." She nods her agreement. "Every single one of them will haunt me. But, until that happens, I'm not ready to stop. I'm ridding the world of scum taking up valuable oxygen."

"And what do you think will happen when someone decides to do the same to you?" She flips her hand dismissively. "It's a serious question. I want to know."

"It won't happen if we work together," is her answer, both simple and effective.

"I'm no longer a cop, I couldn't protect you even if I wanted to."

"You don't have to protect me, Ben."

The conversation isn't progressing the way I want it to. "I don't want to lose you."

"You won't," she says confidently. "I'm good at what I do."

"Trust me, I know that. Damn good. What about if I buy us an island somewhere and we can disappear?" I try to push the point again.

"You honestly can't be so naïve, Ben. No matter where we go, or what we do, at some point someone will come after us. I'd rather be prepared than not. I know I'll be hunted until my last breath, there's no *relaxing*."

There's no use in continuing this conversation, Anna isn't ready to leave her lifestyle behind. "I know," I say as I pick the menu up and pretend to look over it. "I guess, I was clutching at a pipe dream."

"Perhaps one day it can happen, but for now, I have too much work to do to entertain the thought of an easy future."

Maybe my timing is off. I smile at Anna and push her menu toward her. "Maybe one day," I say.

I won't bring this up again. *For a while.*

CHAPTER FIFTEEN

ANNA

The cruise liner has docked in Hawaii and this is our stop. We're going out for a day tour of the Pearl Harbor site, but Ben and I won't return to the liner. We'll be back on the mainland by the time they realize we're not on board, and we'll be long gone by the time any reports are made of the two fictional people who are missing.

"Are you ready?" I ask as we head toward the elevator.

"Sure am."

I connect my Bluetooth earpiece and dial Agent. "Did the newly-weds have fun?" Agent asks, adding a dry chuckle.

"Where are we going?" I'm in no mood for Agent's humor.

"There's a car waiting for you on the end of the Admiral Bernard Chick Clarey Bridge. Black town car. I'll send you the tags. It'll take you to a hangar where a jet's waiting to return you to the mainland. There's a BMW waiting for you at the mainland hangar, you know where the fob will be."

"What happened at the brothel? The girls?"

"Two died from overdoses."

"Damn it," I whisper. "The others?"

"Family came forward for three, and two returned to the streets. The money was distributed per your request."

"And the owners?"

"Investigation is open, and it made the news too."

"It did?"

"That kind of gruesome death isn't normal in Australia, and it's been all over the news. Mind you, there are a lot of theories, but nothing involving you."

"And Katsuo?"

"Not a word on any of the news channels. Cleaner was vacationing in Manila, so he's had his ear close to the ground. The Yakuza found Vang, and disposed of the body. They put it down to Vang wronging someone, and have closed that chapter."

I end the call with a tsk as Ben and I make our way off the ship. "What is it?" Ben asks. I flick my gaze to the crowds as they leave the ship. "A couple of things." I'm disappointed that two of those poor women died, but there's nothing I can do about any of it. I dealt with the monsters who were keeping the invisible shackles on them. There's nothing more for me to do. The survivors need to help themselves.

"There's a black town car waiting for us." I look down at my phone as a text comes through with the tags of the car. With our fingers linked together, Ben and I walk toward where the car should be waiting. "North side, at the end of the bridge," I say to Ben and jut my chin toward a line of cars. "Here."

"Good afternoon. No luggage today?" the driver asks as we approach him.

My skin crawls with the ever-so-familiar feeling and knowledge of something being off. "Wait," I whisper to Ben.

"What is it?"

"Shit, did we forget our camera?" I say to Ben.

"I thought you had it," Ben replies. "Do we need it?"

"Yeah, of course we do." I smile to driver and roll my eyes. "We'll be back in ten minutes."

The driver's shoulders pull back as his eyes widen and he looks around. "I'm sure I can find you a camera."

"Mine's a professional one," Ben says and turns to me. "I didn't even realize you didn't take it."

"We won't be long." With a quick step we turn and head back toward the Pearl Harbor site.

"What the hell is going on?" Ben whispers.

I touch my earpiece. "The car at the dock, did you follow protocol?"

I pull Ben toward a tourist-heavy area. "I didn't deviate from it."

"We've been compromised." How the hell did that happen?

"Where are you?" Agent asks.

"On Kamehameha Highway. Get us out of here."

"How do you know we've been made?" Ben asks as we duck and stay hidden from whoever is after us.

"The driver. He spoke. They never speak, at all. It's one of my conditions." With nimble fingers I swipe two hats from a small tourist store with a hat stand out front. "We need a bathroom."

"Shit." The urgency in Ben's voice has me looking toward him. Two men in suits are quickly approaching us.

"Is there a car close by?" I ask Agent.

"ETA two minutes."

"In two minutes we could be dead." We're moving with the crowds, in the middle of it as we try to stay ahead of whoever is following us. Is it the old gray-haired guy? The Yakuza? Someone else? *Fuck.*

"Café Rosetta, does it have a back entrance?" I ask Agent as I try to make a plan for how we're going to get out of here.

The clicking of the keyboard is furious as Agent checks the design of the café. "There is," Agent confirms. "You have to head out through the kitchen to get to the back entrance."

"Have the car meet us there."

We enter the café and the waitress is speaking with a group of people, taking their orders. Another server heads to the pass-through, balances four plates, and heads over to another table. It's busy in here, which means we can use it to our benefit.

I tug Ben toward the kitchen, where the two chefs look toward us. "I'm sorry to interrupt, but the girl in the front said there's a bathroom out back? I'm not feeling well, and there are so many people out there." I grip the edge of the counter for added effect.

Ben places his hand on my stomach and whispers, "It's early, but this is how we lost the last two. Can we..." He points toward the back.

I want to smack Ben. Pregnant? He has me pregnant? *Seriously.*

"Of course," one of the chefs says as he steps forward. "Can I call someone for you? Would you like some water?" I shake my head and offer him a small smile. He opens the door to the back, allowing Ben and me to leave.

The problem is the door to the alleyway has been boarded off. Probably because they'd had people leave before they've paid. "Fuck," Ben grumbles. He opens the door to the clean bathroom. "We're stuck."

"No, we're not." I pointedly look at the small window above the toilet. I get up on the toilet and peer outside. There's a bank of air conditioning units just below the window, so it wouldn't even be a large drop. "We can do this."

"I can't fit through there."

I step back and scan Ben's body. "The widest part of your body is your shoulders. Come on." We close and lock the bathroom door behind us. It's not large, but we have to make it work. I remove the window pane easily and push out the screen. "When you go out, lift your right arm first, then maneuver your shoulders out. It's gonna be tight, but you should be able to get out."

Ben stands in the small bathroom rubbing his hand across his chin. "I'll buy you more time." He shuffles back toward the door.

"What are you doing?"

"I won't fit, Anna. My shoulders are too broad, there's no way I can get through there."

I jump down off the toilet and grab him by the shirt. "If you don't go, then I don't go."

"You have to get out of here."

"Then get your ass up there and make it work," I demand. Ben bites on his inner cheek, then huffs. "You can sulk as much as you want. Get it done."

"Give me a minute."

"We don't have a minute." He hops up on the toilet, takes a breath, and attempts to get out of the window. I watch as he tries to manipulate his body to get out. "Drop your shoulder," I instruct.

"I'm trying," he snaps with frustration. I use my weight to try and push him through. Slowly, there's movement and he's getting through. "Fuck."

"What is it?"

"Nothing." He pulls himself through the window, and judging by the blood on it, I assume he's hurt himself. I'd rather have him hurt than dead. "Here." He squats and holds his hand out for me.

I pull myself up and wiggle through the small opening. Ben grabs me and hauls me out of the window. He's cradling his left arm, and I notice the gash running from the top of his shoulder to midway between his elbow.

"You okay?" I ask once I jump down and dust myself off.

"I'll be fine."

I look down the alleyway in case a car is waiting. "You there?" I ask Agent.

"I'm here."

"Color of the car?"

"White."

As soon as he answers, a white car turns the corner and slows down beside us. We open the back door, and I make sure Ben is in before I slide in beside him. Ben's breathing is quick, and he lays his head on the head rest and closes his eyes. The car launches and maneuvers around dumpsters down the narrow alleyway onto the main street. I look behind us to make sure no one is following; it appears all clear.

"Are you okay?" I ask as I tear at the bottom of my shirt, and wrap it around Ben's arm to stop the bleeding. A person on the street catches my attention in my peripheral vision. The woman is looking around, trying to find someone.

She's trying to find us.

Adele.

"She would've detained you if I was not here." The driver has a strong, familiar accent.

The old gray-haired guy.

What the fuck is going on?

"Agent," I say and wait for a response.

"Phones and tracking devices not work in this car."

"Who the fuck *are* you?"

"There is small medical kit in the back. Stitch him up so he doesn't bleed out." He points over his shoulder to the fold-down arm rest between the seats. I pull it down to find a small, yet adequate, first aid kit.

The saline is buried at the bottom, but I retrieve it and snap the lid off. I pour it over Ben's wound. "Shit," Ben grumbles and closes his eyes. He must be in quite a bit of pain, although it's not life-threatening. He's had worse.

"Who are you?" I ask as I clean the wound and find the surgical needle and thread. "This is going to hurt."

"Great." Ben expels a humorless chuckle. "Fucking great," he repeats.

"A simple 'thank you' will do," the old man says.

"Fuck you," I say as I pinch the skin together and pierce the needle through Ben's arm.

"Fuck!"

"Shut up and let me stitch you."

"It hurts."

"So does a slow painful death by bleeding out." Ben grinds his jaw together and snarls. But he takes a sharp breath and closes his eyes. "Where are you taking us?" There's a small pair of surgical scissors in the medical kit that I place under my hip. I'll kill this fucker if he doesn't tell me who he is or where we're going.

"To my hangar so I can take you back to the mainland."

I hate not knowing what's happening. But if this fucker doesn't talk soon, the scissors under my hip will be in his throat. "Why are you doing this?" If he tells me the *why*, I should be able to work out the *who*.

"I told you. You and your sister are very important to me."

Fucking riddles. "Why?" I stab the needle into Ben too aggressively, and he reaches out and grips my thigh. "Sorry," I whisper.

"When you reunite with your sister, I will tell you."

"Reunite?" As in I've already met her. "Do I know who she is?"

"*Da*," he says proudly.

I stop stitching and look over at him. "What?" Ben asks as he opens his eyes and glances between me and the old gray-haired man. "They know each other?"

"What the fuck?" I'm going to lose my shit soon, and I hate losing control. Losing control is a weakness, and I'm not fucking weak. Never have been, never will be. I glance up and notice how far the old man has managed to get us from Pearl Harbor.

"When we get to the mainland, I'll explain everything."

"Or alternatively, you could tell us now," I say, ready to shove the damn scissors into his throat.

"I no can tell you now."

Of course he can't. I finish stitching Ben and dress his wound. Ben relaxes against the seat and it's clear he's relieved I'm no longer working on him. "You okay?" I ask Ben who offers me a nod as his reply. The old man zooms through the rolling hills, and I'm left with more questions than ever.

The car ride is quiet from here on in, I'm in no mood to speak to either him or Ben. I just need to think. The old man navigates the streets until we reach a hangar where his jet is waiting on the tarmac.

The moment I'm out of the car, I touch my earpiece, connecting me to Agent.

"Where are you? Your GPS dropped out. I'm tracking you now."

"Ben and I are about to board a plane to take us to the mainland."

"I've got you. That's not where our plane is located."

I look over to the old guy who's strutting toward the jet. "I know." I touch my pocket to confirm the scissors are still in there. "We'll be fine."

"Do you need me to send Doctor or Cleaner?"

There's a strong feeling in my gut that the old man is a friendly and won't harm us. He's had ample opportunity so far and hasn't acted upon it. Besides, a pair of scissors severing the jugular vein can put him down. But I have a feeling he's been around my kind for a lot longer than I have.

"Neither is needed. Do you have the pedophiles? Is there an extraction team ready to grab them?"

"On your go-ahead," he confirms.

"Go on that. Send me the location where they're being held by the time we land on the mainland."

"On it."

I end the call and walk over to Ben. Ben clears his throat and he looks over his shoulder toward the jet. He shifts his posture and clears his throat. "I'm uneasy about this."

"So am I," I reply. "But something is telling me everything will be okay."

He glances at his bandaged arm. "I'm not sure what good I'll be to you if you need me."

"I've got this," I affirm and pat my pocket to double-check the scissors are still safely in there. "Agent's lining the pedophiles up for me."

"Anna, Ben," the old man calls from the top of the stairs. "We need to leave." He gestures for us to come on board.

"You sure about this?" Ben asks.

My steps hesitate. "Nope." But I continue heading toward the jet. Ben jogs ahead of me, putting himself at risk in case there's a threat on the jet.

Gallant gesture, but I'm the one who can protect us. "Wait here," he says before taking off into the jet to check things out. He returns only a handful of seconds later. "You're good."

How cute, he'd put himself in danger for me. I climb the stairs and head into the jet. "Welcome," the old man says as he holds his hand out with a glass of something to me. "Scotch." He thrusts the glass closer, but I don't take it.

He may have proven that he isn't an enemy, but I can't be too careful. Ben grabs the glass and downs it in one fluid motion. "What are you doing?"

"I'll be the one affected if it's drugged."

"You very suspicious," the old man says with a sly grin before sitting and looking out the window. "I don't blame you. I'd be suspicious too."

I touch my earpiece and I'm surprised to find it connects to Agent. "What do you need?"

"Where are we landing?" I ask the old man.

"Where you want to land?" His thick accent is easily understandable even though his words are short and broken.

"Where are the pedophiles?" I ask Agent.

"Oh, more torture. I watch, *da*?" The old man perks up with eagerness.

"Where do you want them?" Agent asks.

Ben sits on the other side of the aisle to the old man, and lays his head back against the seat. I look to him, and he smiles before taking a deep breath and closing his eyes. The drink wasn't drugged, which is comforting to know. I'm not going to have to kill the old man. *Yet.*

"I have place you can use. Nice and quiet," the old man adds.

"Prepare for takeoff," the captain says over the speaker.

"Where is it?" I ask.

The old man gives me of the address of his building and I convey it to Agent. I also give him a list of tools I'll require. I hang up and sit beside Ben. The old man is across the aisle from me, nursing his own scotch. I'm being led around by someone I don't know, and I'm forced to trust him. Trust that he won't kill me. Trust that he won't turn me in to the authorities. Trust that he is an ally and not an enemy.

For now, it'll have to do. But I won't hesitate to put the scissors through his neck if he double-crosses me.

I look around the jet and find the absence of any bodyguards unnerving. If he had a cadre of guards, I'd know the sort of person he is.

Maybe he gets his kicks out of watching people die.

I have no idea.

Fuck, my mind is a whirlwind of unanswered questions.

I'll find out who he is soon enough. But for now, I'll sit back and watch everything about him.

CHAPTER SIXTEEN

ANNA

Knock.

Knock, knock.

I walk over to the door of the hotel where we're staying and open it. Doctor looks past me. "Where is he?" He barges in armed with his fedora and medical bag.

"He's in the shower."

Doctor walks in and places his medical bag on the table. He takes off his fedora and fans himself. "It's hotter than Satan's asshole down here, and it shouldn't be this hot considering the season."

"It's not as bad as Sydney was." I walk over to the fridge and take two bottles of water out, handing one to Doctor. "Two of the girls died from an overdose."

"I'm aware." He takes the lid of the water off and consumes a third of the bottle. "How are you? Cravings?"

"Yep," I truthfully reply.

He visually scans my arms. "You're not using."

"No, I'm not."

"It wasn't a question. I know you're not."

The water turns off, and within a minute, Ben strolls out in just a towel. "Oh." He startles when he sees Doctor.

"Get dressed," Doctor instructs.

Ben disappears into the bedroom and reappears dressed in jeans with no t-shirt. "I thought you'd be here later."

"Sit." Doctor points. "Who stitched you?"

"I did," I say.

"How did it happen?"

"Window," Ben replies.

Doctor removes the now-wet bandage from his arm. "You need to keep this dry and covered." Ben winces as Doctor removes the last part of the bandaging. "You'll need a tetanus shot, and I'll give you some antibiotics too." Doctor looks in his medical bag and takes out his glasses. He pushes them up the bridge of his nose. "You stitched him, 15?"

"I did."

"Huh." He carefully assesses the wound and slowly nods. "Look here." He gestures for me to look at the wound. "These three stitches are good. They're tight and nicely spaced, but these two are quite messy. If you're ever in the position that you have to do stitches, keep them like this."

"Will they have to be redone?" Ben asks. "Because if so, you need to give me a pain blocker."

"Did you do them without anesthetic?"

"I didn't have access to any," I reply.

"Then you did an above average job." Doctor sounds impressed. Surprising really, because Doctor is never impressed by anything. "I won't need to redo the stitches. They'll suffice." He rummages through his bag and produces a syringe, ointment and new dressings. "Keep it dry." Doctor cleans the wound and applies the ointment on it. "Put this on it before it's wrapped." He quickly wraps it, then draws medicine into the syringe. He stands and walks around to Ben's other side and jabs it into his arm. "This'll hurt by tomorrow, and you'll likely have a small bump. Don't worry about it; it'll go down." He caps the syringe, then removes a bottle of pills from his bag. "Take these, two a day with food. Antibiotics. Take them for ten days. Before you ask, it's a precaution more than anything else."

"Thank you," Ben says as he stands.

"Is there anything else?" Doctor looks to me and waits.

"Nothing else."

He closes his medical bag, picks up his fedora, then heads to the door. "Agent has me here until you leave." He fans himself again and takes a breath. I take it Doctor isn't a fan of the South. He places his hat back on his head and leaves the hotel room.

"I think he wants to get out of here," Ben says.

"I should keep him down here longer."

Ben snickers as he walks into the room and returns with a t-shirt. "When are we heading out?"

"Soon. First, I need to take a shower." I walk into the bedroom and strip before I head to the bathroom.

The building blends into the others lined up beside it. "No one will bother you here," the old man says when the car stops. "I own it all."

It's a strip of industrial buildings, with people milling around some of the ones toward the front. "They all work for you?"

"*Da*," he answers. This is the first time I've seen his men. One of them holds the door open and waits for the old man to enter. "This way." He leads us into the building.

Ben links our hands together and steps ahead of me, following the old man. The guard holding the door open is staring ahead, completely stoic. I walk in and the guard follows, closing the door behind him.

The moment I'm inside, I hear a pained moan coming from deeper in the cold room. I scan the room to assess everything going on. Toward the back, there's a St. Andrew's cross with an Asian man strapped to it. How amusing, something used for pleasure is now being used for indescribable and horrid pain. His naked, broken body appears to have already been beaten. His head is hanging low and blood steadily drips down his leg to the floor.

Opposite him, there's a table with an array of knives, guns, surgical equipment, and a small propane torch.

"Do you need more?" the old man asks as he runs his fingertips over the weapons.

"This is sufficient." I look around the room. "Where are the other two?"

The old man looks to the guard who was on door duty. He walks into the darkness and returns with both of the other guys. They appear terrified. *Good.* "Where you want?"

"Over there, on their knees." I want them positioned in front of the cross so they can watch what I'm about to do. Three guards line themselves up in front of the table so the two pedophiles can't dive and make a grab for any of my weapons.

The old man sits in a chair. Ben drags another chair over and sits beside the two on their knees.

I approach the man cuffed to the cross. I lift his chin to stare into his eyes. "Who are you?" he asks in a small pained voice.

"That doesn't matter," I reply. "Do you know why you're here?"

He shakes his head and bursts into tears. "Please, you've got the wrong person." They're all whimpering cowards when the tables are turned.

I snicker and inhale loudly. "They always say that."

"I don't know you," he screams. "I haven't done anything to you."

"You haven't done anything?"

"No, I haven't. P-p-please," he begs between sobs.

"I'm going to give you the opportunity to die fast or slow. The choice is yours, and yours alone."

"I don't want to die," he hysterically screams. Spittle sprays from his mouth as a long line of drool follows.

"We're beyond that now. You are going to die today." I clap a hand to his shoulder and squeeze. "Now, tell me why I have you here and I'll kill you quickly."

"I don't know. I haven't done anything."

"My audience wants to see me work. Now they get their wish." I walk over to the table and run my hand over all the weapons. I lift a metal pipe and smack it a few times in my hand.

"No, no, p-please," he begs. "I know why I'm here."

I turn to face him. With the metal pipe still in my hand, I walk over to him while carefully keeping an eye on the two sniveling idiots kneeling on the ground. "Why?"

He sucks in a deep breath and lowers his head. "Be-because." For fuck's sake, get on with it. "I like little girls."

"There it is. You *do* know why you're here." I swing the metal pipe and smash it across his left kneecap. He cries out in pain.

The cracking of the bones vibrates and causes me to smile a satisfied grin. "P-please."

"Do you need something?" I smash the pipe across his groin, knowing the pain would be crippling.

"I b-beg you."

"You beg me for what?"

"Kill me, please k-kill me."

"How many little girls begged you to stop?" I smash the pipe into his other knee. His high-pitched scream delights me to my very core.

"How many times did they beg you to stop and you kept going?" He lifts his chin to look at me, silently pleading to end his life. I swing the pipe toward his face, but stop just before it makes contact. "I lied, I'm not going to kill you fast." Fucking scum deserves the pain.

I look over to the two kneeling and smile. "Please," one begs.

"Do you know why you're here?" They both nod. "Why?" I walk over to the table and place the pipe down, lifting a hunting knife.

"I touched that little girl," the one kneeling closest to me whimpers.

"That's right." I slit his throat. Blood spurts out as he collapses to the floor. "And you?" I ask the other one quivering in fear.

"I...I..." He lowers his head in shame.

The one up on the cross inhales sharply, reminding me not to forget about him. I take the propane torch and light it. "You what?"

The guy kneeling crumples to the floor, blubbering his meaningless apology. "I'm sorry," he cries.

"So you should be." The guard who was at the door is standing nearby. I flick my hand to him so he lifts him from his collapsed state. The guard fists his hair and yanks him up. "Stop hyperventilating," I say as I shake my head. I walk over and squat beside him. "You had to know someone was going to come for you one day."

He shakes his head vehemently. "I was protected by Vang."

Just the mention of his name causes a reaction to fester deep inside my gut. "Vang's dead." His brows pull in together and he audibly swallows. "You didn't know he was dead?" He shakes his head. "Want to know a little secret?" He keeps staring at me, not responding. I lean in and whisper, "I killed him." His eyes widen. "Slowly." In one fluid motion, I grab the hair on his head and bring the propane torch up to his face. He screams as the torch burns him. The stench of burning skin fills the air.

"Well done," the old man says as he crosses his legs and watches.

I pull the torch away and stand to my feet. I replace the torch with a Glock. Just feeling the weight of it tells me it's empty. I check the magazine and shake my head. "Really?" I say to the old man, who's smiling proudly.

Asshole, it was a test.

I lift the second Glock, and from the weight, I know it's loaded. I walk over to the guy who's screaming in agonizing pain and angle a bullet through the top of his head.

"You are..." The old man brings his fingers to his lips and kisses them. "What they say? Chef's kiss?"

"Please," the guy on the cross begs.

"I almost forgot about you," I say. I lift the hunting knife and walk over to him. I stab it into his ribs deep enough to know I've punctured his lungs. "You're going to suffocate in your own blood."

I turn and walk away from him. "I'm sorry, I'm sorry," he cries.

"I don't accept your apology. I'll see you in hell." I walk over and stand beside Ben. We watch as the beast on the cross loses his battle and takes his last breaths. Nothing brings me more joy than seeing a cruel piece of shit put down.

"Wonderful!" the old man says as he claps his hands. "You are beautiful and bloodthirsty."

I look around the room and assess the fact his men have me out-numbered. I won't be able to kill all of them, but I'll be able to take him out if he doesn't tell me who he is. "Who are you?" A small smile tugs at his lips as he moves to stand. I move quickly to push him down so he can't leave. "No, you're not going anywhere."

I hear the click of many guns and turn to see not one of them is pointed at me. They're all directed toward Ben. The old man sucks in a large breath and gestures for his team to lower their guns. "*Da*, it is time."

"If this is another game..."

"*Nyet*." He waves his hand at me. "I am your grandfather, Anna."

"Shit," Ben murmurs.

I straighten my shoulders and nod. I thought we were related; I had that feeling niggling at me since we met. The fact he said my sister and I are important to him should've been an indicator, and in truth it was. But, now I'm sure. I know we're related. I don't need any more proof. But I'm also not an idiot. I won't blindly accept his words. "You're my grandfather?"

"*Da*."

"Who are you?" I stand rooted to the spot with my arms crossed defensively in front of my chest.

"My name is Dmitri Petrov."

"Petrov is a common Russian surname. A quarter of the population has it."

"*Da*," he confirms with a cheeky grin.

"What name do they whisper in fear?"

He throws his head back and laughs. "You very smart." He shakes a long, skinny finger at me. I continue to stare at him, holding in any emotions I may be experiencing. I need to know who this man is. He stretches his arms over his head and then relaxes. "Yakovich."

I look to Ben, then back to the old man. "As in Siyalov Yakovich?"

"*Da*," he confirms easily.

"But…" I uncross my arms and drag a chair to sit opposite the old man.

"*Da*." He nods.

"The rumors were that Siyalov Yakovich was killed by one of his own men, leaving the bratva to fall into disarray."

"They were the rumors, *da*."

"If you're Siyalov Yakovich, then why…?" I shake my head as I attempt to piece it all together. I look down at the floor, then back to Ben. Neither of us have any idea what's happening. "I don't understand," I finally admit. "Did you fake your death? I mean, why would you do that?"

"It's very difficult question." Dmitri taps his finger against his mouth.

"Does this mean the business didn't fall apart? The Yakovich bratva is rumored to have lost its clout, and people are no longer afraid of the name. But." I point to Dmitri. "I don't understand. Why do that?" The Yakovich bratva was beyond powerful. It had a reach into many businesses, making it one of the most successful bratvas in Russian history.

"You must return with me and take your place."

"Take my place?"

"Take her place?" Ben asks at the same time I do.

"What are you talking about?" I ask.

Ben stands and walks over to me, placing his hand on my shoulder. His warmth is reassuring, I know he has my back. "*Da*, you return with me and we make Yakovich name strong again."

"Um, no chance in hell, Dmitri. I work alone."

"Business needs you. Siyalov Yakovich needs you."

My eyes narrow and my jaw tightens. "What aren't you telling me?"

"Come, we go for dinner and we discuss." He stands and reaches his hand out for mine.

I look at his hand, then flick my glance up to him. I turn to Ben and silently ask him what he thinks. He's just as confused as I am. "Sure," Ben says.

"*Nyet*, you no come."

"If Ben doesn't go, neither do I." I link my fingers with Ben's. "Now that I know who you are, I can easily walk away from you. But something tells me you need me. So..." I suck in a deep breath. "Ben is with me, or neither of us go."

Dmitri glances between Ben and me several times before reluctantly agreeing. "*Da*." He waves his hand over his head in resignation.

"Bathroom?"

Dmitri instructs one of his men to show me to the bathroom, where I quickly clean the blood off my hands but notice the amount on my t-shirt. I take my t-shirt off, and walk out to find them all staring at me. "You no go like that," Dmitri spits toward me.

I look down at my black bra and black, skintight pants. The blood on my pants isn't anywhere near as bad as the blood on my shirt. "Yeah, I am."

"No!"

"Are you embarrassed?" I look down at myself again. "Because I'm not."

"You leader of Yakovich, and leader of Yakovich does not wear..." He flicks his hand with disgust. "That."

"I'm 15, and I do whatever the fuck I want," I counter.

"Ilya," Dmitri calls. The guard who was at the door rapidly steps toward us. "Jacket." Ilya removes his suit jacket and hands it over to me. Ilya is older, and quite distinguished, unlike the other men Dmitri has hanging around. It makes me think Ilya means more to Dmitri than the others. *Or, maybe not.*

I cock a brow, then smirk. "Fine." I untie my boots and slip them off, slide my pants down my legs, leaving me in my bra and panties. I speedily put my boots on again, take the jacket and put it on, leaving just two buttons fastened. The jacket is long, and covers my ass. And with my severe ponytail, boots and bra peeking out, I already know I look hot without even needing a mirror to confirm it.

Ben snickers as he runs his hand across his eyes. "Ahhh," Dmitri mumbles his disapproval. "I no sure which is worse."

"Well, you wanted me to cover up. So, here I am, covered." I extend my arms and twirl once. When I turn, I stare at Dmitri with a snicker. *You wanna come at me, old man?*

"Barely."

"Do you want to eat, or not?"

Dmitri sighs and shakes his head. "*Da*, I do."

Ben covers my hand with his and we follow Dmitri out to the waiting car.

We've been in the car for almost half an hour as Dmitri makes small talk telling me nothing about the operations of the Yakovich bratva. I suspect he's going to tell me all about it soon, but for some reason he's waiting.

"I have a question," I say as I shuffle closer to Ben.

"*Da?*"

In truth I have a million questions, but I'll start with something relatively easy. "When I asked you who you were and it became a little heated, all the guns were pointed to Ben, and not one of them on me. Why?"

The old man pours himself a vodka in the back of the limousine and sips on it. "He mean nothing. You my granddaughter." Thought as much. "No one touch you."

Ben's hand tightens around mine. "Here's the thing. If your men do anything to Ben, then you and I have a problem."

Dmitri's eyes widen before he licks his lips and takes another sip of his vodka. He lowers his glass and clears his throat. "Understood," he concedes. "Vodka?" He lifts the bottle to show me.

"I'm a scotch woman."

"You learn to be vodka woman." I lift a brow and turn away, essentially telling him what I think about that.

The rest of the drive is spent in silence. The car pulls up curbside and the driver exits first, then opens the door for us. Dmitri slides out, leaving Ben and me in the car. "You okay?" I ask in a low voice.

"Why wouldn't I be?" He moves across the seat and climbs out of the car, then holds his hand out to me. I take it and look around.

I know this place. The Second Moonrise is Frankie DeLuca's restaurant. One she uses to launder money. I completely respect her, and how shrewd she is as a mob boss. She's employed my services a few times, and I've never had a problem with her.

"Come," Dmitri says as he offers his elbow for me.

Ben instantly releases my hand and indicates for me to walk in with Dmitri. "Sir," the man at the door greets. "Ma'am." He looks me up and down and arches a brow.

The restaurant is busy with people dressed in expensive suits and dresses. Some recognize me, and tip their head in respect. Some are repulsed by my attire, which makes me smile.

"You're such a wallflower," Ben whispers. I pull my shoulders back and lift my chin, owning my presence. After all, I'm 15.

"Sir," the maître d' says. "The VIP area is ready." She leads us to the back, where we have an entire room to ourselves. It's like a mini version of the dining area out the front. The restaurant is fitted out in opulent dark colors and low mood lighting.

Once we're all seated, the server is already pouring us water. "Scotch," Dmitri announces and pushes the water away. *Good, he's learning*. The waitress wordlessly leaves the room. "My men have already swept the room. You're more than welcome to look it over yourself."

"I have no reason to doubt you." I stare at Dmitri and add, "So far."

The server returns with a bottle of top-shelf scotch and begins pouring us each one. Again, like a ghost, she leaves the room, leaving the bottle behind. Ilya's hard presence is guarding the door, his guns proudly displayed in holsters. Is he Dmitri's henchman? Personal bodyguard? He appears to be nearly everywhere Dmitri is. "Drink." Dmitri pushes my glass closer to me.

"Why are we here?" I ask, ignoring the scotch.

"Food. *Da*, you're hungry?" He turns to Ilya and flicks his wrist at him. I sit back in my seat and place my hand on Ben's thigh. He rests his hand over mine and we remain a united front. "Siyalov Yakovich isn't exactly what people expect." Dmitri knots his bushy, gray brows together.

"Go on," I urge. It's like pulling teeth with this guy; he gives me only dribbles of information.

Dmitri looks around, pours himself another drink, and downs it. He places the glass on the table and turns to me. "Siyalov Yakovich was never me."

"What? Then who are you?" This makes no sense at all.

"We made it look like it was me, but it wasn't."

"Why?"

"Because it was expected that a man be the head of the family."

"Well, who's Yakovich?" Ben asks as he leans forward, invested in what Dmitri is going to say.

"The head of the family was my sister."

"Was?" I ask. "What happened to her?"

"Ovarian cancer," Dmitri says in a small voice. "It was too late when it was found."

"Shit," I whisper. "But, what does this have to do with the business?"

"Our father knew the bratva wouldn't accept a woman as the leader, so I played the part in public but she was the real head."

"Well, now you're the real head of the business," I say. "So, I don't understand what you want with me," I pause for a second as I think about it. "Or my sister."

"I'm sick, and I will die soon." My brows rise as I nod. "I want my granddaughters to keep going."

"Ilya can do it," I say, already not interested in taking over the bratva for my Russian grandfather, nor interested in whatever illness he has.

"No, it needs you." I glance over to Ilya who's returned and is back at his door position. He appears completely emotionless. "You are so much like my sister. Cold, ruthless, savage, unforgiving."

"I'm sure you have others who can take the reins."

He begins to chuckle. "When we little kids." He holds his hand out to the side, indicating height. "She would find bird with broken wing, and she'd snap its neck. She'd say, 'Dmitri, bird is sick and better to kill it than let it suffer.'"

"She's not wrong."

"*Da*."

"What about my grandmother, your...wife?" I don't want to make an assumption but we're talking about old times and traditions.

"She was...what you call? Hooker."

"My grandmother worked as a prostitute?"

"*Da*, she worked as prostitute I could have whenever I wanted. My father found out she was pregnant and sent her to America. I only found out I had a daughter when my father died."

He never knew about Natalia? What is going on? "What?"

There's a knock on the door, which Ilya opens. Several servers enter, all holding share plates. "Perog, pelmeni, syrniki, goulash, and borodinksy bread," our female server announces before leaving with the rest of the staff.

Russian food in an Italian restaurant. Got it, Dmitri had already organized this ahead of time. "I don't understand. When did you find out about Natalia?"

"When I found out, I came to America and tracked her down. She was married, and had a baby—you. She left you in the hospital and disappeared, for what reason, I don't know. I never talked to Natalia, but I found out she became involved with drugs shortly after abandoning you."

"So you knew where she was? You knew where I was?"

"*Da*, I kept an eye on you." He wets his lips and shakes his head. "I didn't know they were going to take you or kill your father. When my men found out, I came to find you, but you had killed the kidnappers and had disappeared. I couldn't find you."

"Why didn't you..." I swallow the lump in my throat. "Why didn't you knock on my door when you knew I was alive?" His eyes well as he sits back and clears his throat. "Why? Why wouldn't you show up, knock on my fucking door, and tell me you're my grandfather?"

"I knew you were being looked after by Harry."

"You should've been there," I say, finding my own anger is escalating. I need to calm before I lose it with him.

"It's okay," Ben whispers as he tightens his hand over mine.

"No, it's not okay. He knew about me and never bothered to reach out to me. My father would've been alive if you had your men looking after me."

"Anna," Ben says.

"Fuck this." I stand and leave the room, Ben behind me. "I need a minute," I say to him over my shoulder.

"No, you need to calm down."

I swing around and stare at him. "Don't you fucking tell me to calm down. I need to get out of here." I pivot to make a swift exit, but Ben reaches out and grabs me by the upper arm, stopping me. "Let me go." I can easily overpower him, but I need to remember he's not my enemy. "My father would be alive if it wasn't for him."

"Are you sure?"

I step backward until I find the wall. "What do you mean?"

"I never knew Harry, but everyone at Bankstown Creek would tell me how much he loved his daughter and how fiercely protective he was. Do you really think Harry wouldn't fight tooth and nail with Dmitri to keep him away from you? And then what do you think would've happened? Dmitri would've taken you from your father, and you would've hated him. He did the best thing for you by letting you live your life with Harry."

I lean my head back against the wall and close my eyes. I take several deep breaths, just like Dad taught me before I open my eyes and nod at Ben. "I guess you're right."

"Let's go back in and hear whatever else Dmitri has to say." Ben holds his hand out for me and waits until I take it. "This isn't a normal custody battle situation. Your father was a cop, and your grandfather is the head of a Russian bratva. It's probably best he left you, because you weren't a threat for him then. Can you imagine if his enemies found out about you? They'd kill you and your father without even blinking an eye."

My breath is even, but my mind is spinning with the knowledge that Dmitri *maybe* could've prevented my father's death. I don't know what to think. We head back into the restaurant, where Dmitri is pacing back and forth. With my usual level of arrogance, I return to my seat and wait until Dmitri sits. "What happened when you found out about Dad and me?" I ask in a composed tone.

"I came immediately, and got to the house while it was still burning. We then found the car, and the two dead men."

"By we, I assume you mean you and your man who was supposed to be watching?"

Dmitri nods and lowers his chin. "He did not do good job. I killed him." Is that supposed to make me forgive Dmitri? "But, I saw what you did to those two men, and knew I had to bring you to live with me—train you for the business. So, I put the word out to find you."

"Clearly you didn't."

"I did," he admits easily.

"You knew where I was?"

"*Da*, Lukas reached out to let me know he had you."

"You left me—a fifteen-year-old kid—to fend for myself?"

Calm the fuck down, Anna. Just breathe.

"*Da*, Lukas once worked for me, and so he gave me reports. He told me about your progress, and I left you with him to train, to look after. But..."

"I killed him," I say.

"*Da*. The man you killed was your final test, Lukas was going to bring you to me. But..." He lifts his brows and tilts his head to the side. *I killed him.* "Then, you disappeared and I didn't know where you were. But, you rose quickly and became a force. And, I kept an eye on you. Most times you disappear, but you would always show up somewhere."

"Did you know Vang had me?"

"At first *nyet*, but we found you through him." He points to Ben.

"Me?" Ben asks.

"How's Ben involved?"

"Because I knew you take out Mancini family, and we have few members of police on the payroll. They told us about Ben and the warrant for him, and knew he'd be looking for you. So, we followed him. I then found Vang had you, and Ben was looking for you." He lifts his scotch and takes another sip. "One of Vang's men is FBI."

"Who?" I ask.

"You have FBI on your team too," Dmitri says to Ben.

"At the station?" Ben asks.

"*Da.*" Dmitri nods once.

"Someone at the station is FBI?" Ben repeats with skepticism. "*My* station?"

"Bankstown Creek, *da.*" Dmitri nods with confidence.

"Who?"

Dmitri's face screws up as he slowly lifts his shoulders. "That is a little difficult."

"Wait," I say. "Who on Vang's crew was FBI?"

"His name is Tyler." He clicks his fingers several times as he tries to recall his surname. "Lewis. *Da*, Lewis."

I'm not even surprised. Tyler kept trying to get me away from Katsuo before the raid. Of course. It makes perfect sense. "What about at the station?" I ask, completely moving on from Tyler.

"Um." His brows furrow as he swirls the remains of his scotch around in his glass. "Adele," he says.

"Adele?" Ben's pitch rises. "Adele?" he repeats. "But I ran a check on her, made sure she was clean because I didn't want another Mancini situation on my hands. She was clean."

Dmitri's eyes widen as his lips thin into a closed, tight smile. "What else aren't you telling us?" I ask.

"Adele is…" He clicks his tongue to the roof of his mouth.

My mind is speeding ahead. I have a feeling I know what he's about to say. But I have to hear it from him first. "She's what?" I ask as I wet my lips and stare at him. My heart rate increases and my pulse quickens. I grip Ben's thigh. "What?" I repeat slower.

"Adele Petrov."

Adele Petrov. As in Dmitri Petrov. As in…my sister.

Silence blankets the room as I blankly stare at Dmitri.

"What the fuck?" Ben says in a small voice.

My sentiments exactly.

CHAPTER SEVENTEEN

BEN

"It's kind of strange, don't you think?" Anna asks as we sit out on the balcony of the hotel, sipping a beer.

"What part exactly do you think is strange?"

She looks up into the inky night sky and lifts her beer to her mouth. "I have relatives. A grandfather and a sister. My sister is a cop, actually an FBI agent, and my grandfather heads up one of the largest criminal organizations in Russia, maybe even the world, albeit it's not at powerhouse status anymore."

I snicker as I lift my beer to my lips. "Kind of strange?" I ask with sarcasm.

"Can we be any more different? I'm an assassin, Dmitri is bratva, Adele is FBI and you're an arms dealer."

"I'm out," I break the news to Anna.

She lowers her beer and slowly turns to stare at me. "You're out?"

"We touched on this when we were returning from Sydney. I'm going to leave everything to Emily, and step away from it all."

"Wow." She shakes her head as she brings the beer to her lips. She instantly lowers it without drinking any and turns to me again. "How fucking irresponsible of you."

"Irresponsible?" I turn my body in the chair to look at her. "What?"

"You're throwing away all the work and sacrifices your family has made. Your parents and your sister died, and you're throwing in the towel?"

"I'm not throwing in the towel. I'm trying to be responsible by getting out of the game."

"And that's responsible, is it? Tell me," she starts, placing the beer bottle on the floor. She stares at me. "What part of this is responsible? You're an arms dealer who refuses to sell weapons. Do you know what'll happen when it gets out that the Pace family is falling apart? Emily will be killed, then they'll come after you. If anything, you need to amp up your presence and let the world know you're Ben fucking Pace. You don't take shit from anyone, and if someone comes for you, you deal with them. Stepping away will never be an option while we still breathe."

I lower my head to look at the top of my bottle. "I don't want Emily or you to die because of me."

"You need to forget about whatever idea of perfection you have in your head, and focus on reality. Emily needs you, and you need Emily. Neither one of you can do this on your own. You need each other."

"You don't have anyone," I say to Anna.

"That's different," she almost whispers. "I've been on my own since I was fifteen, besides, I have Agent."

I narrow my eyes at her, stand, and walk over to lean against the railing. "You also have me."

"Do I?" She stands and approaches me. "Two minutes ago you were about to turn your back on your family. How can I trust you won't turn your back on me when you were going to give up your rightful legacy so easily?"

Fuck, I never thought about it like that. "I wanted to get out to protect you and Emily."

"By leaving us in danger," she points out. "Ben, the businesses we're in are full of danger. It would be nice to know someone has my back, someone I don't pay. And, you know, if anything goes south for you and Emily, you have the world's best sharpshooter available to you." She steps closer and wraps her arms around my waist. I kiss the top of her head. "For a price," she adds with a lighter tone.

"You'd charge me?" I bring her closer to my body, pressing my hard cock into her.

"I'd obviously instruct Agent to give you a discount."

I chuckle and shake my head. "A part of me actually believes you would charge me." She doesn't reply with a laugh. Now I'm seriously questioning it. "Would you?" I slightly push her back so I can read her face.

The corner of her lip trembles as she holds back a laugh. *I think.*

"So, it's settled. No more bullshit about you walking away."

"I'm not going anywhere." Anna's lip twitches again. "I think we need to talk about Dmitri though."

"I've been wrestling with my thoughts about him."

"He dropped a lot on you earlier at dinner. There's so much to think about," I say while linking our fingers and heading back to our chairs. I pick Anna's beer up and offer it to her, then take mine before sitting beside her.

Anna sips her beer, then places it back on the floor. Absentmindedly, Anna begins twirling the end of her hair with her fingers as she stares out over the rooftops. "I don't know what to do," she finally admits.

"Not to mention, your sister is a cop. FBI no less."

"I can tell you one thing for sure."

"What?" I ask.

"*She's* not going to take over for Dmitri. No chance in hell. I won't let her."

"It's not your choice, Anna. It's hers."

"No way," she adamantly replies. "No fucking way is she being introduced to this side of the law. Nope." She waggles her finger at me, before inhaling deeply and returning her attention to the rooftops.

"Dmitri will attempt to recruit her, if it means the bratva will be run by you and her."

Anna's jaw tightens while she stares into the night. I notice she begins rubbing her fingertips together as she gazes out at nothing in particular. Anna shakes her head. "No. I don't like this."

"It's up to Adele, not you."

"We both know this world is ruthless, as is Dmitri. I have a bad feeling about this."

"As in what?"

"Something's telling me, he'll do anything to get what he wants. And by anything, I'm sure he wouldn't think twice about ripping her away from her family, even if that includes destroying them. Wait." She crinkles her brows and turns to face me. "Do you know if she has a family?"

I recall back to the background check I had Emily run on her. "When she initially started at the station, I wanted to make sure I didn't have another Ethan on my hands."

"As you've previously stated."

I silence her with a glare. She chuckles. *Smart-ass.* "As I was saying, before you rudely interrupted me." She wobbles her head and gives me an eye roll. "She came up with a clean record. She was adopted when she was young, and nothing was suspicious about the parents. They won a massive lottery prize when they were younger and have since invested in the housing market and live off the income from that. Essentially, they're retired."

Anna nibbles on the inside of her cheek and her shoulders slump forward slightly. She's worried, and rightfully so. Dmitri has come into her life like a wrecking ball, and now he's demanding her attention and her time. But not only that, he wants her sister too. "What's she like?"

"Adele?"

"No, Mother Theresa." She shakes her head.

"She's a hard worker, but as we both know she's FBI, so she had a role to play."

"She couldn't have joined the FBI if she wasn't capable," Anna says. "She's clearly able to do the work." She purses her lips together and takes a sharp breath. "I don't want this life for her."

"It's not up to you. She's an adult."

"Yeah, she is." Anna wrings her hands together and shakes her head at the same time. She's thinking, and I know whatever she's going to suggest will result in her putting herself at risk. *Again*. "As much as I want a sister and a real family, I can't let her do this. It's not the world for her."

"We're going around and around in circles here, Anna. It's not up to you."

"No, it isn't, it's up to Adele."

"The only thing you can do is ask her," I furiously throw out.

Anna instantly lifts her chin to look at me. "Ask her?"

"No, I didn't mean that. You should definitely not involve her in this. She's FBI and hunting me, which means it'll only be a matter of time before they figure out who you are. You should *not* go anywhere near her. *Ever*."

Anna jumps to her feet and heads inside. Within a few seconds she's on the phone to Agent. "Can you hack into Adele Petrov's phone?" She licks her lips, then contorts her mouth. "How long?" Anna nods. "As soon as you have a location." Then she disconnects the call.

"What are you planning to do, Anna? Waltzing over to her house and telling her who you are, who your grandfather is, then demanding she ignores it all? Either way this isn't going to go well."

"If I do nothing, you know what Dmitri will do. I'd rather she arrest me than she or her family die. I can handle prison…" She looks down at her feet. "I don't want her to go through what I did when my dad was killed."

I walk over to her and enshroud her with my body, hugging her close to my chest. Anna's resistance to my touch is futile, because I refuse to let her go. She's a hard-ass who refuses to ask for help, but we're in this together now. Regardless of where it leads. "If you really want to do this, then we have no other option but to take her."

"Take her? As in kidnap an FBI agent?" Anna asks. "I'm not opposed to kidnapping a corrupt cop and slicing the bottom of their feet before putting a bullet in their head," her reference to Ethan makes me smile. I thought she was brutal then, but that was nothing in comparison to what she did to Vang. "But she's not corrupt."

"Technically, we're not kidnapping an FBI agent. More like, kidnapping your sister."

"Who happens to be an FBI agent hunting you," she corrects.

"Semantics. Neither here nor there."

Anna releases her arms from my waist and steps backward. She scrubs her hand over her face several times. She's warming to the idea, and truthfully, I'm already formulating a plan to take Adele. "Dmitri can't know anything."

"Who's going to tell him? You or me?" This entire night has spun on its head. I thought I was relinquishing my family legacy, instead I'm formulating a plan to kidnap Anna's half sister, the FBI agent.

"Let's go over the plan." She heads back into the room and turns toward me. "Are you coming?"

Who am I to say no to the woman I love?

Chapter Eighteen

Adele

"**M**omma, I'm home," I call as I close the front door behind me. The delicious aroma of Mom's stroganoff instantly leads me into the kitchen. "Mom?"

"Hey, you." Mom smiles when she sees me. She stops stirring the food and comes over to give me a kiss and a hug. "I didn't know you were coming today."

"It's my day off, and I thought I'd come for dinner. Where's Dad?" I lay my helmet on one of the stools at the kitchen island.

"He's out with Patrick. Good, you can start the pasta." She looks over at the bag of flour sitting on the counter.

"Ugh, really?"

"If you want to eat, then you need to help." I wash my hands and roll up my sleeves. "You remember how, right?"

"Yes," I snap.

"What's wrong?"

I sift the flour and salt onto the kitchen counter and make a well in the middle. "Nothing."

"Nothing?" Mom leans against the counter, watching me. "If you say so."

I crack the eggs into the well and with a fork, begin to incorporate them into the flour, starting from the center and working my way out. "I have a question."

"What is it?"

I don't know how to broach the subject. I'm hesitant to ask, because every time I do, I've pretty much been shut down. The pasta is starting to form a doughy consistency, and I continue kneading it until it's smooth. "I need you to tell me what you know about my birth mother."

Mom flinches and straightens. "I..."

"Please, I know you know something, because every time I asked when I was younger, you'd shut me down. And, I know you know something about her, because I was eleven when you adopted me and you never even met me before you decided to adopt me."

Mom turns and stirs the pots on the stove. "We don't know much about her."

"Please don't lie to me," I beg. "I just want to know what you know about her." I watch Mom as I continue to knead the dough. "Please."

"I don't know anything," she says in a cold, hard tone.

Everything inside me tells me she does know something. "Mom?" I repeat. "I just need to know something...anything?"

"Maybe your father knows something. Wait until he returns and ask him."

"Fine, I will."

"Good," Mom says. "I can't help you." In my gut, I know Mom is lying. She's holding something back. "Keep an eye on the range, I need to go to the bathroom." Mom ducks out while I knead the pasta into the beautiful consistency it needs for noodles. I wrap it in cling wrap, place it in the fridge, and wipe down the counter. Mom's been gone a while. I stir the pot on the range, then decide to find Mom. As I approach her room, I hear her whispering. The door is closed, so I can't make out too much, but I swear I hear her say, "We're going to have to tell her before she finds out for herself." She's talking about me.

I knew it. I knew that my parents know more than they've told me.

If they're not ready to tell me about my birth mother, Dad's going to avoid coming home until after I leave. Which means I'm not going anywhere until they tell me everything.

I back away and return to the kitchen. "Everything okay?" I ask when Mom rejoins me, knowing whatever she's going to say is either a lie or a cover-up.

"Of course." Mom startles as her phone audibly rings. Mistake number one. She always has her phone on silent. So it must be Dad who's going to give an excuse as to why he can't return home tonight. "Oh, it's your father." She swipes across the screen. "Darling, how are you and Pat doing?" She listens for a second and exhales. "Oh that's terrible. Adele's here, and she was hoping to speak with you." She listens again, then says, "Hang on. I'll put you on speaker."

They can't avoid me forever. "Hey, Dad," I say, keeping my voice even.

"Hey, sweetheart, I didn't know you were coming over today."

"It was a spur of the moment decision. Anyway, when will you be home? I just made fresh pasta and Mom's making stroganoff." Here comes the excuse.

"Oh no. I don't think I'll be home until tomorrow. Pat's boat needs some repairs and I'm staying to help him."

"Damn it, Dad. Really?" I'm so disappointed with his obvious lie. How many more lies have my parents carelessly told? This is making me question so much.

"Yeah. I'll be home tomorrow morning, but I just don't think I'll be there before you leave."

"Oh well, we'll catch up next time." I'm not going anywhere. "I'll probably leave right after dinner, because I have work tomorrow." I actually don't, so I'm staying until we talk.

"I was hoping to see my little girl." He's trying to convince me with false remorse.

"Yeah, me too. Anyway, say hi to Pat for me."

"Will do. Love you."

"Love you too, Dad."

Mom reaches for the phone and takes if off speaker. They speak for a few moments, before she hangs up and slides the phone back into her pocket. "What a shame your father couldn't be here."

"Yeah, such a shame," I say in a voice heavy with sarcasm.

The thing is, I'm persistent. I'll get my answers, one way or another.

"Sweetheart, it's late. Don't you have work tomorrow?" Mom asks as she settles into her armchair with a cup of tea.

"Yeah, I do. I should head off now." My plan is to leave, wait for half an hour, then return. That should give Dad enough time to come home. "I'm so comfortable here. Maybe I should stay the night."

"But you don't have your work stuff here." She's trying to usher me out so Dad can come home. How bad can the past be that they have to hide from me?

I bounced around in the system until they adopted me. Did something happen to me because of my mother? Did my mother do something to me so I was taken away from her? What's the big secret? "Yeah, you're right. I better head home then." I push up off the sofa and stretch my arms up over my head. I walk over to Mom and give her a kiss on the cheek. "Thanks for dinner, although I made the pasta."

Mom brings the mug to her lips and blows on her hot tea. She smiles, then takes a sip. "Maybe you should move back in. It's nice having a live-in chef available."

"Yeah, yeah." I roll my eyes as I grab my motorcycle keys off the hook behind the front door and retrieve my helmet from the stool. "Bye, Mom."

Mom places her mug on the coffee table, then stands with groans and moans. "I'm getting too old for this."

"For standing?"

"I need one of those electric chairs that tilt up and you get to your feet easily."

I turn to look at her and raise my brows. "Mom, you've only just turned fifty. You're not that old."

"I feel it after I've been sitting then I have to stand." She gives me a kiss and sees me to the door. "Love you."

"Love you too." I head over to my bike and place my helmet on. I start the bike and carefully look around in case Dad is waiting for me to leave.

As I ride toward home, I decide to pull into a twenty-four hour fast food establishment to grab a coffee and wait.

I park my bike, walk in, and order a coffee.

I can't help but think about what they're hiding. Was I a child of molestation or rape and they don't want to tell me about it? Was I trafficked? Abused? Sold? What can be so bad that Dad's avoiding me?

I want answers. Regardless of how horror filled or traumatic they are for me. I need to know where I came from, who I am, who my birth parents were.

Maybe they believe I'll think less of them, but they'll always be my parents. They adopted me when no one wanted me. They loved me, even though I wasn't their natural child. And for that, I'm eternally thankful.

I look down at my coffee and notice I've already drunk it all. I've been so stuck in my head that I hadn't realized I'd been drinking it.

Is this the calm before the storm?

If so, whose storm is it? Mine? My birth mother's? My parents?

I know something monumental is about to happen, but I need to know who she was. It might explain who I am too.

"Thank you," I call to the waitress as I throw a ten on the table.

"Have a good night," she responds as she heads over to take my cup and the money.

I push through the door, walk over to my bike, start it, and head back over to my parents'.

A humorless chuckle escapes me when I see Dad's car in the driveway. I was right. He was waiting for me to leave before he returned home. I park two houses up and carefully sneak my way to the front door. Muffled voices are coming from within. I make out my name, but nothing more than that. As quietly as I can, I use my copy of the front door key to enter.

Mom and Dad are in the kitchen and haven't heard me come in. With my helmet in my hand, I walk into the kitchen. Mom startles when she sees me, and Dad turns on the spot to see who it is. "Adele, what are you doing here?" Mom asks with her hand over her chest.

"Adele," Dad says as he looks to Mom, then back to me.

"Mom had no idea I was coming back," I say. "But, now that I'm here, it's time you tell me what you know about my mother."

"Oh boy," Dad exhales as rubs at his eyes.

"Do you know anything about her?" His silence and Mom's pained look tells me they both do. "Look…" I walk over and pull out a stool. "It's not like you know who killed her." Mom bites on her lower lip as she turns away, and Dad groans. Wait, they do know?

"Why is this so important?" Dad asks.

"Really?" I slump on the chair. "All I know is she was shot, that's it. I want to know about her, and I want you to be the ones to tell me if you know anything. I'm going to find out, but I prefer to hear it from you."

"Tell her," Mom says.

I look to Dad and shuffle toward the edge of the barstool. This is it. I'm going to find out something about her. Shit, is this what I really want? I clasp my hands together to stop the tremble. "I need to know more about her if I'm going to find who killed her," I say.

"She was assassinated at the ballet," Dad says.

"By a sniper, along with her husband who ran something like a mercenary for hire business. I keep coming up empty past that though, other than her name was Natalia Murphy. Nothing before she became Natalia Murphy though, it's almost like she was a ghost before she became his wife. I need answers." I look down at the counter and shake my head. "Please," I shamelessly beg. "Anything."

Dad angles his head from one side to the other, and a loud crack booms when he stretches his neck. "It's complicated…"

"I don't care how complicated this is. I just need to know." I move to take both Mom and Dad's hand but there's a loud knock on the door. "Are you expecting someone?" Who'd be showing up this late?

Mom and Dad look to each other. "No, no one," Mom says.

"Stay here." I walk over to the door and angle my body to the side. I creak it open and someone knocks into the door, forcing me to stumble backward. My eyes land on Ben Pearson and I reach for my gun. That's locked away in my safe at home. Fuck. "You're under arrest," I yell. "Get on the floor."

Anna charges in behind him holding two guns and pointing them at me.

"What's going on..." Dad's voice instantly stops. "Anna?"

"Ilya?" she asks with her guns still pointed.

I look between everyone as I attempt to put this all together. "Ilya?" I ask. "Who the fuck is Ilya?" There's a dreadful moment of silence in my parents' home. "What the fuck is going on?"

Anna flicks her guns to make us walk backward. "Get back." She's standing tall, her eyes wild. I have no doubt she'll pull the trigger if necessary.

I hold my hands up in surrender to calm her. "We're doing what you want." I glance at Mom and Dad over my shoulder to check on them and find neither are stressed by this. "Wait." I lower my hands as I step backward.

Ben closes and locks the front door before moving past us and arranging three dining chairs in the middle of the room away from everything. *Smart.* "Do what they want, sweetheart," Dad says.

"Sit." Anna gestures to the chairs with her guns before aiming them back toward us.

Dad sits in the middle, I sit to his left and Mom to his right. He links his hands with mine and Mom's. I'm so confused as to how they know each other, or even what's going on. "Can someone explain to me what is happening here?" If Anna and Ben are here, does that mean Katsuo Vang is somewhere nearby? Are they all in this together? And again, how does she know my father?

"It's time we tell you about your family," Dad says with a resigned sigh.

What is going on?

CHAPTER NINETEEN

— · —

ANNA

I did *not* see that one coming. Fuck, this is one intricate web of lies. Ilya is Adele's father. But, how? Why?

This certainly took a turn I wasn't expecting. Not to mention the fact they live less than two hours from Bankstown Creek. How is it possible that they've been here all this time, and I've never known? Easy. I didn't know about them and had no reason to look for them.

Ilya shakes his head and exhales. "It's time we tell you about your family."

"I have no idea what's going on, except I need to arrest Ben," Adele says.

"That's not going to happen," I say with certainty and a tinge of mirth that she thinks she'll even be able to arrest either of us. She's outgunned here.

Adele's eyes are wide, though the deep crevices in her forehead tell me she's trying to piece this together. "Your grandmother came to America when she was pregnant with your mother," Ilya relays the parts I already know to Adele. "She was a prostitute who became pregnant by someone important."

I let him tell the story while keeping my guns trained on them. Ben stands to the side in case one of them wants to make a run for it.

"So, my grandmother was a prostitute?"

I nod, as does Ilya. "She had Natalia and when Natalia was about fourteen or fifteen your grandmother died. And Natalia took to the streets for a little while but she cleaned herself up and got a respectable job. Then she met a man, and married him."

"So far, I'm keeping up," Adele says, then sneaks a look over at me.

"They had a child."

"I have a sibling?" Adele asks with overwhelming interest. "Are they alive? Do you know where they are? Do you know where I can find them? Do you have a name?"

Ilya holds his hand up, stopping Adele from asking any more questions. Fuck, I'm so nervous. I feel like I'm about to be sick. He's going to tell her about me, and I'm holding a gun on her and her family. There's a fluttering in my stomach and a tingle prickling my skin. Is Adele going to freak out? "You have a sister."

"A sister? Where is she? Is she alive? Can I meet her?"

Jesus, the tension is fucking killing me. Ilya takes a deep breath and lowers his head. He lifts it and flicks a look to me. "Yeah, you can," he says as he's staring at me.

"When?" Adele asks. Again, silence overtakes us, and it's in the next moments of silence that she puts it all together. "You're my sister," Adele whispers as she slowly turns toward me.

A part of me wants to lower my guns and throw my arms around her. But she needs to know all of it. Every last detail before any kind of healing can start. Especially for Adele. "Tell her all of it," I instruct Ilya.

"But..." his protest is met with my staunch glare.

"All of it."

"Oh boy," Ilya's wife whispers. Wait, there's more to this story that I don't know? Judging by the tears in her eyes, I think there's a lot more.

"Natalia married Harry, but the call of being a free spirit was too strong for her. And after she had Anna, she simply vanished. She didn't want the pressures of being a mother, or a wife."

"What a saint," Adele says the words I've always thought about our dearest mother.

"She turned back to her familiar life, in the streets. She became an addict and did whatever was necessary in order to survive on the streets. We don't know who your father is, Adele. We put it down to a pimp or a john."

"That's awful," Adele responds with her hand to her chest.

"You were born an addict," Ilya says.

"What? I was? Why didn't you ever tell me?"

"You were bounced from foster home to foster home before your grandfather discovered he even had a daughter. He came to America to find Natalia, but she was in the streets."

"Wait." Adele holds her hand up. "I have a grandfather?" Ilya nods. "But he found his granddaughters. Kind of." He pointedly looks to me. "He knew of you both, and he found you in the system."

"Why didn't he come for me?" Adele's voice softens. "Didn't he want me?" She looks over to me. "Us? Didn't he want us?" She points to herself, then me.

"He missed Anna by hours. Her father was killed, she was kidnapped, and her house was on fire when he got to her home. When he did discover where she was, he left her with the man she was with."

"Ewww." Adele screws her nose up. "How old was she?" She looks to me. "How old were you?"

This is where the story is going to get difficult, but she needs to know everything. "I was fifteen."

"You were with a man at fifteen? Oh my God, I could've protected you. We could've protected each other."

"It wasn't like that," I say.

"What was it like then?"

She watches me for answers, but I look to Ilya. "Keep talking, Ilya."

"Why is she calling you that name?"

Ilya releases his wife's hand and runs it through his hair. "You have a lot of questions, and if you can wait, you'll know all the answers." Adele closes her mouth and nods her agreement. "He didn't take you to live with him because he couldn't care for you, and he lived a dangerous life."

"Dangerous?"

"Your mother and I have been your parents and legal guardians since he found you. Our instructions were to keep you safe until it was time for you to take over the family business, when we'd tell you everything, and you and Anna would step into the power."

Something about Ilya tells me he doesn't want Adele in this life any more than I do. I think he actually loves her like a daughter.

"Power? I don't want power," Adele says. "Do you?" she asks as she turns to look at me.

"I already have it."

"You're running this business I have no idea about?"

"No, I've made a name for myself doing something else."

"What name?"

She needs to continue with our family history, especially about Natalia before I tell her who I am. "Ilya, tell her about Natalia and Hunter Inc."

"Hunter Incorporated? The guns for hire? What's she got to do with them?"

"When Natalia was strung out, she was paid in the form of drugs, to try and kill Lincoln Murphy. He went on to head Hunter after his father was killed. He saw potential in Natalia, and he took her off the streets, cleaned her up and taught her."

"Taught her what?" Adele asks.

"How to kill people," I say.

Adele's head whips around to look at me. "You're kidding, right?"

"Not at all," Ben interjects and stands taller.

"How do you fit into all of this?" Adele makes a circular motion with her fingers around me, Ben, and her father and mother.

"There's more you need to know," Ilya says. He looks to me to continue with what my part is in all of this and where Ben fits into it.

"My father was killed the day I turned fifteen. Two men were sent to kidnap me, and obliterate anything that stood in their way. They knew my father would hunt them down, so they blew his brains out while I watched."

"Oh my God," Adele whispers as she lifts her hands to cup her mouth in horror. "Why would someone want you at such a young age? For sex trafficking? To be a drug mule?"

I love how innocent she is, it also proves to me that she doesn't belong in our world. "I had a particular skill set, and the person who gave the orders to take me wanted that skill set."

"What on earth can a fifteen-year-old be skilled in?" She gawks between us, waiting for the answer.

"I'm an expert with weapons."

Adele looks at me and slowly lifts her shoulders. "What does that even mean?" She stares at me, waiting for an answer. "Are you going to tell me?"

"Let me tell you who I am, first."

She grits her teeth and clicks her tongue, frustrated. "I know who you are. Anna Moore."

"That's what she wanted you to think," Ben says.

Adele fidgets in her seat before crossing her arms in front of her chest. "I'm sick of all of this. If you're not Anna Moore, then who are you?"

"Anna Moore is one of my aliases. My father was Harry Brookes." Adele slowly uncrosses her arms before she sits forward and glances around the room. "As in the former police chief of Bankstown Creek," I add.

"He died in a house fire."

"Not before he was executed in front of me."

"But it was presumed you had died."

"Uh-huh. As my kidnappers intended," I say, still aiming my guns toward her and her parents. "But I killed the men who were sent to take me as we were driving away. I put bullets into their heads. Then I made it my mission to find the man who gave those orders, and kill him."

"I completely understand the need for justice. I want the same thing for Natalia." Ben looks over to me and gives me a small nod to continue with the story. "But how? You were just a kid. How did you know how to handle a gun like that?"

"I told you, I had a particular skill set. Dad taught me from an early age how to safely use a gun. I was—*am* good with targets. *Really good*," I add with a small humorless chuckle. "But I happened on a man who trained me further. So, I reinvented myself."

"Reinvented?" she repeats. "As who?" I need to deliver the blow to her fairy-tale life. "Who did you transform into?"

Here goes. She's about to hear a name she's probably heard in her years as a cop and FBI agent. A name whispered in fear by so many. "My name is..." I pause, unsure this is the right path. But she has to know who her family is first. Then I have to convince her not to follow our grandfather's wishes to head up the Yakovich bratva. "15."

I let the name sink in for a long moment. Adele's mouth gapes open while she shakes her head in denial. "What? 15 is a ghost, an urban legend."

I love that's how people think of me. "15 is very real." Ben says.

"You're an assassin?" Adele grips the edge of the seat, stopping herself from standing.

"I am."

"There are so many rumors about 15. The FBI has never been able to confirm the identity, even though 15 is on our most wanted list.

"You're one of the most ruthless assassins in the world. It's rumored you can take a target out at three miles."

"Why am I always so severely underestimated?" I ask Ben.

"Over three miles?" Adele asks.

"That's beside the point."

"It is, because now I have to arrest you." My shoulders slightly slump. Does she honestly believe she stands a chance with me? "But, there's still so much more I want to know. Like, how does this circle back to my—*our*—mother? And him?" She pointedly stares at Ben.

"The man who gave the orders to take me and kill my father was Ronan Murphy."

"Lincoln Murphy's father," she says. "He took over the business after his father died."

"After I killed Ronan."

"That kill was done while he was in a moving car. One shot to the forehead." She lifts her hand and rubs at the spot between her eyebrows.

"Yeah, it was," I confirm.

"You did that?" I nod. "Okay, but what does this have to do with everything else. As far as I'm concerned, you saved us from having to arrest him." She doesn't appear too fazed by my admission. "And our mother factors into this how?"

"Lincoln sent her to kill Ben."

"What? Why? That doesn't make sense. Ben is a cop."

"*Was,*" he says quite forcefully. Adele turns to look at him. "I *was* a cop." She then swings her attention back to me.

"But, why? Why send an assassin to kill Ben?" she asks.

"Because of Ethan Martelli."

"My predecessor," Adele says. "He disappeared, and no one knows where he is."

"I killed him," I say. "I also killed his father."

"What? Why?"

"Ethan Martelli's real name was Anthony Mancini Jr. He and his father had a cocaine refining plant running just outside of Bankstown Creek. The Mancinis killed Ben's parents as a warning, then they indirectly tried to bribe him. But he didn't take the bribe. So, the Mancinis paid me to kill him."

She flicks a look to me, then Ben. "Clearly you didn't kill him."

"Obviously. But Mancini Sr., Ethan's father, hired a secondary assassin through Hunter Inc. to take him out."

"Natalia," Adele says in a small voice.

"Natalia," I confirm.

She takes a deep breath as she lowers her chin to think about what I've said. "There's got to be more. Because this is too intricate for it to stop there."

"Because I took out Murphy's men who were sent to take me, Murphy put a bounty on my head. After I killed Murphy, Lincoln kept the bounty, until I negotiated a new deal."

"New deal?"

"It was a deal that I wouldn't kill Lincoln if he withdrew the bounty. When he reinstated it, I killed him at the ballet." I leave it at that, because Adele is going to quickly piece it together.

"Natalia died beside Lincoln," she says in a small voice. It doesn't take her long to look up at me. While shaking her head, unbelieving what she's thinking, she asks, "Did you kill Natalia, your own mother?"

"Yes," I say. There's no reason to hide the truth now.

"Because of the bounty?"

"That's why I killed Lincoln. Besides, he wanted to recruit me and he thought he was better than me. But, that's not the reason I killed Natalia."

"Then why?"

"Because she came after Ben and tried to kill him. And she had a gun pointed at me the whole time while I conducted my negotiations with Lincoln."

"Kill or be killed," Adele says.

"Something like that," I reply.

She looks to Ben and lets her gaze wander the room. "You did this for Ben?"

"I did this because I could. She was a threat to me, and I remove anything that has the capacity to weaken me."

Adele mistakes my admission for a threat. "Are you going to kill me?" She looks to her parents. "My mom and dad?"

"I have no intention of harming you, Adele," I answer honestly.

"There's more you need to know," Ilya says.

Adele closes her eyes and rubs her hand across the bridge of her nose. "This is quite overwhelming," she says. "But..." She swallows and lowers her hand. "What else do I need to know?"

"You know your mother and I won the lottery years ago?"

"Just before you adopted me."

"We didn't win the lottery. That was a lie."

"What?" Adele jumps to her feet. "Is my entire life a lie?"

"Of course not," her mother says and rises to instantly wrap her arms around Adele.

"Nope, we're not doing this," I say as I indicate to Ben to pull them apart and have them sit.

Adele stares at me with a wide mouth. "Come on, this is a lot for me to handle."

"You can hug and kiss and do whatever the fuck you want to once we're gone."

She turns to her father and takes his hand in hers. "Where has the money come from then?"

I hate how we're corrupting Adele, then we're going to force her to keep our secrets. Or she's going to hunt us. *All of us.* "From Pat."

"Pat?"

"Pat's name isn't Pat," Ilya says.

"Who is he?"

"Dmitri Petrov." Ilya hangs his head and closes his eyes. He rubs at his temples.

Adele's face drains of color as she sits back in her seat. "*He's* my grandfather?" her small voice is barely audible. "And you're who to me? To him?"

"I work with and for Dmitri. We've been friends for many years."

Adele stands abruptly, prompting Ben to straighten and use his body to push her back toward her seat. "I need a fucking drink, because this is crazy. My entire life has been nothing but a fucking lie."

"Let her go," I say to Ben. He steps aside but follows her to make sure she doesn't try anything. I don't want to be put in a situation where I have to shoot her. I will, but I'll make it a flesh wound, nothing that will kill her.

Adele walks over to the fridge, opens it, and grabs a beer. She flicks the lid off and gulps the beer in one go, releasing a huge burp. "Let me get this straight." She looks to Ilya, "What you're telling me is the man I've known for years to be Pat, is actually my grandfather, who's funded this elaborate life of lies I've lived." She looks to me and says, "You're the sister I had no idea I had and you're single-handedly one of—if not *the most*—dangerous assassins in the world. You also killed our mother because she was also an assassin? After she abandoned you when you were a baby to run off and become a junkie. Am I getting this right?"

"Essentially you've summed it all up fairly nicely," I confirm, adding a small humorless chuckle.

She rubs her hand across her forehead and leans against the kitchen counter. "Is there anything else I need to know about this circus? Do I have a brother anywhere? Or maybe a long-lost fucking twin somewhere?"

"There's more," Ilya says.

"Oh, I can't wait for this," Adele replies with an elevated voice. "What more could you spring on me?"

"Adele, you need to calm down," I say.

"Calm down? Are you fucking serious?" She shakes her head in disbelief. "I'm not even sure...I can't..." her words are jumbled with confusion. "Fuck." She turns and opens the cabinet above the fridge and reaches for a bottle of tequila. She unscrews the lid and takes a long drink from the bottle, then holds it out to me. "How the fuck do you sleep knowing all of this?"

"I only found out about your relationship with Ilya tonight." I reach for the bottle and take a sip.

"If I have any more of that, I'll lose my shit." Adele snatches the bottle from me and places it on the counter.

"There's something you need to know about our grandfather."

Adele let's out a long grumble as she rolls her head backward. "I'm not sure I can take too much more."

"Dmitri also works under another name." Adele lifts her head to look at me. Her mouth is open and a fine sheen of sweat beads across her hairline. "Ilya is one of his bodyguards."

"I don't even want to ask, but why does he need a bodyguard?" She looks over to me. "You said *one* of his bodyguards?"

"Because Dmitri is Siyalov Yakovich," I say.

Adele slowly licks her lips before she begins to laugh. She quickly stops and straightens her shoulders. Her exterior is quite composed given everything we've told her. "Russian mob boss," she says.

As an act of good faith, I lower my weapons, resting them against my thighs. Ilya notices this immediately and his eyes widen. "I don't want to kill you, so don't," I warn. "Dmitri expects us to take over his organization."

"What? Why?"

"Because he's not well," Ilya says. "And he needs you both to work together and advance the bratva."

"Why don't you run it and leave me out of it?" Adele asks. "I can't even believe I said that out loud," she murmurs as she lowers her chin and blows out a deep breath. "I'm fucking FBI. How am I supposed to go to work and not tell them everything I know?"

"I don't want it either, Adele. And I don't want it for you. You can't cross the line over to this side, because once you do, there's no going back. Ever."

"I feel sick," she says as she holds her hand over her mouth. The room is silent once again. Adele lowers her hand and looks at me. "You killed my mother."

"*Our* mother," I correct.

"And our grandfather knows this?"

"Yes," Ilya confirms.

"This is...crazy!"

"It's a lot. But you don't have to make a decision tonight," Ilya says.

Both Adele and I look over at him. "She's not doing it," I say. "There's no decision to make."

"Hey, you don't speak for me," Adele argues.

"You're not doing it." I hold my hand up to her.

"You don't know me, Anna, and you can't make a decision for me."

"We share the same bloodline, Adele. We're both killers, but you do it on your side of the law." I tap my chest. "I make my own laws, and live by my own rules. You don't belong in my world."

There's already a deep-rooted connection between us, regardless of the fact we're the opposite sides of the same coin. She's light and good, I'm dark and merciless. She has no darkness in her, and I have no light in me.

We *could* make it work. Together we'd be an unstoppable force of nature. Like a tsunami, a fire, an avalanche, and a tornado all combined. We could absolutely rule the underground.

But there's no way I'm going to allow Adele to join this side. She's too pure a person to live with herself if she had to kill someone to protect me, and I wouldn't even ask her to do it.

"I need a few days to wrap my head around this and give..." She opens her mouth and closes it again while shaking her head like she's attempting to dislodge a thought. "...our grandfather my decision."

The room is again filled with silence. "You don't have to do this," her mother says.

"What choice do I have?" Adele replies. "This is my legacy."

"No, it's not," I add. "If anything, it's my legacy and not yours."

"If I don't join you, then I have to tell work about you, and you." She looks to her father. "And everything about me."

"No, you don't," I say.

"How am I supposed to keep this from my superiors?"

"It's called family secrets," I say.

"I work for the God damned government! I *arrest* people like all of you." She points to her father, Ben, and me. "I need some time." Adele shifts her weight from foot to foot, unable to keep still.

"No, you don't. You're not going to do this. I won't allow it."

"Who do you think you are?"

"I'm looking out for my little sister," I say.

"I'll hunt you down."

"Pffft," I chortle. "There's no conviction in your voice, so I know you'll never look for me. But, if you need me, I'll give you a way to contact me."

"I'll track it, and I'll find you."

"You won't have to look hard, because I'll always be watching."

"Stop treating me like a child!" she demands and even adds a foot stomp for extra emphasis. I arch a brow as I stare at her.

Adele squirms and huffs several times. "You'll resent yourself if you choose to do this. But, besides that, you'll resent them too." I point to her parents.

Her shoulders tighten and she pokes her tongue into her cheek. "I'm not sure I'll be able to stop that from happening either way." She swallows and looks over to her parents.

Both her parents lower their chins in embarrassment. Good, so they should for never telling her the truth. "It's settled," I say as I tuck both my guns into my waistband. "You're not to become involved in the bratva."

"Anna," Ilya says. "Let Dmitri have his say."

"Have his say?" Adele interrupts. "He's had a chance to do that ever since I was brought here to live under the guise of finding a family. He could've spoken up at any time. It's only now that Anna's found me that you think Dmitri deserves to have his say. If anything, the only person in this room I trust at this moment is Anna. And she's a fucking assassin." Adele is quickly becoming emotional. "I'll speak with Pat...Dmitri..." Her brows crinkle. "Grandfather and tell him I can't be part of whatever he wants me to do."

Thank God she made that decision on her own. "No, I'll break the news to him," I say. I jerk my head to the side so Ben and I can leave. "Goodbye, Adele," I say as I step backward toward the front door.

"Wait." She makes the move toward me, and Ben places his body between us.

"Ben." My tone urges him to step aside.

She walks around him and comes to stand toe to toe with me. Her cheeks turn pink and her eyes brim with tears. Adele brings her hand up to lightly pinch her lower lip while she continues to stare at me. She's hasn't said a word. Her own internal struggle must be waging its own war. Her brows pull in, her nose wrinkles, and her eyes redden even further. "I have a sister," she whispers.

"You do," I reply. My own emotions are caught in my throat. But I have to be strong, because she can *never* be a part of my life.

She begins to reach out to me, but lowers her hand and steps back. "I..." Adele's battle is stopping her from saying what she needs. "Thank you," she finally says. "For telling me the truth, for giving me a family, and for..." Agony spreads across her face.

I get it, she never wanted to make this decision, and I somewhat took it out of her hands. She doesn't want this life, nor do I want it *for* her. "Don't mention it," I say, knowing the words would be difficult to express.

"I'm not sure what I'm going to do about you, though."

I snicker as I step backward. "Good luck with that."

"If I'm ordered to come after you, I'll have no choice."

I chuckle a little louder. "Like I said, good luck with that."

"Aren't you scared?"

"Of you?" I point to her, then shake my head. "You're my sister." I lift one shoulder and wink. "I'll have a phone delivered to you, if you ever need me, call the number on the phone and I'll find you."

"What if I use it to catch you?"

Any normal person would be consumed with worry that their law enforcement sister would arrest them, but she won't do that to me. There's a lightness in my chest telling me I have nothing to worry about from her. I lift my chin higher and pull my shoulders back.

"You won't. But, until we meet again, Adele." I give her a small head nod. "It's good to know I have a sister who's nothing like me."

She steps forward, and Ben protectively uses his body to shield us. "This is where we leave you," Ben says. "It's best you stay inside."

I turn my back on them and exit through the front door. Ben's heavy footsteps quickly follow. He forces his fingers into mine and links our hands together. We get into the car and drive away.

"Are you okay?" Ben asks.

"I will be, once I set a meeting with Dmitri." The drive toward my cabin gives me time to plan on how the meeting will proceed.

"What are you going to do?"

"I have a gut feeling that things will work themselves out. But I may need to give it a helping hand to work out the way I want it to."

Ben tsks with a smile. "I guess. We'll see how things turn out."

I'll call Dmitri and set a meeting with him. "Yep," I say as I speed toward my cabin.

Chapter Twenty

Anna

"Dmitri," I greet as Ben and I walk into his hotel suite.

He walks over to me and kisses me on both cheeks. This takes me aback, because I had no idea we were at that stage. "Come, come," he says as he walks over to the cabinet filled with hard liquor and pours three scotches. He offers one to Ben but Ben waves his hand, refusing it. "*Nyet*?"

"It's too early for me," Ben jokingly replies.

Dmitri hands me the glass, and I take it. "It's five o'clock somewhere," I say as I throw the two fingers of scotch back.

"I have vodka if you want?" Dmitri offers Ben. Ben waves away the second offer too. "You here to discuss offer, *da*?" Dmitri sits on the arm chair opposite the sofa. "Sit." He gestures for me to sit on the sofa.

Ilya stands at the door with his shoulders back and chin high so he can see Dmitri's back. Ben stands to my right, where he has a clear view of all of us. If this goes how I plan it to go, then neither Ben nor I will need to show our guns. "I am," I reply to Dmitri.

"Good. We fly out tomorrow after we take your sister."

I notice Ilya's upper lip twitch when Dmitri mentions Adele. It's also interesting to see that Ilya hasn't told Dmitri about our meeting two days ago, or Dmitri would already know Adele isn't going to be part of this. "Nope." I sit back and cross my legs while extending both of my arms along the back of the sofa. "I won't be taking over, and neither will Adele."

Dmitri clearly doesn't like what I've said. He stretches his neck and straightens in his seat. "You spoke with Adele?"

I shake my head. "I don't need to, I've made this decision for her. She's not in our line of work, and she never will be."

Dmitri runs his tongue over his teeth before relaxing. He lifts his brows and sucks in a deep breath. "You will both take over," he says with finality.

I glance to Ben, then over to Ilya. Ben clasps his hands in front of him, and Ilya carefully watches Ben in case he goes for his guns. Interesting; Ilya and Dmitri have to know I can take them both before their hearts beat once. Maybe Ilya isn't going to respond the way I was hoping, which means I need to execute plan B. I'll give him one more chance before I put bullets between their eyes.

"No. Like I said, Adele and I are out. Pass the business on to someone else."

Dmitri calmy says, "I think it's in Adele's best interest if you do take over."

I don't need to look at Ilya to see his reaction. He shifts his position slightly, his lips part and he bores his hard stare at the back of Dmitri's head. Hmmm, it appears I won't need to draw my weapons after all. "Or what?" I ask casually.

"I tell him to kill you, and he will." Dmitri juts his head back toward Ilya.

"You'd kill me?" Like Ilya would stand a chance against me.

"*Da.* You are what bratva needs, so you will take your place beside me."

Huh, interesting. It's gone from taking over the bratva, to standing beside him. He needs a henchman, and he thinks he can use me to do his dirty work. Sorry, buddy, I'm no one's puppet. "Kill me." I shrug nonchalantly. "Go ahead."

Dmitri's face hardens, his nostrils flare, and his eyes narrow. The tension in the room is growing as he stares at me with fury. "I kill Adele to teach you lesson."

Ilya's upper lip twitches as he quickly turns his cynical gaze toward Dmitri.

I suck in a deep breath and forcefully stand. Dmitri startles but quickly regains his composure. "Good luck with that," I say.

"You leave, I kill her," Dmitri declares in his hard Russian accent.

I throw my arms up in surrender. "Do what you must."

"I will torture her."

"Great, do you need some tips?" Ilya cracks a tiny smile, while Ben quickly moves beside me, keeping his eyes are on both Ilya and Dmitri. "Gentlemen," I say and give both Ilya and Dmitri a small nod before Ben and I leave the hotel suite.

Dmitri thinks he can use Adele to control me. "Well, that was interesting. Do you think it'll work?" Ben asks as we wait for the elevator.

I look over to him and smile. "Did you not see?"

"I saw how angry Dmitri was."

I look back to the suite and smile. "I have a good feeling."

Ilya

"Call Adele," Dmitri spits with hatred and anger. "Bring her to me."

"Why?" I ask.

Dmitri turns and stares at me. "Because that girl is going to take her place." He points toward the door of the suite. "If I sacrifice Adele for her, then so be it."

There's a roaring in my ears as I watch Dmitri pace back and forth. "That may set Anna off to kill you."

"Ungrateful whore," he bellows not even listening to me. "Who the hell does she think she is?"

"15," I say with a touch of humor.

"You think this is funny? If Anna does not take her place, then the bratva will die. My family legacy will die."

"I don't think killing Adele will make her change her mind."

"I will strip everything away from her. She will have no choice but to come to me, and to take her place." He stops pacing and turns to me. Lifting his finger, he waves it at me furiously. "Starting with Adele. Once Adele is finished, then we move to Ben. I don't care, I will burn the world and she will take her place." He starts pacing again while he runs his hand through his hair. "Bring her here. I need Anna to see I mean business. I call Anna back and slit Adele's throat in front of her. She will know, she must take her place beside me."

I can feel my own scowl grow as Dmitri speaks of Adele like she's nothing more than a rag doll. "Dmitri—"

"No!" he snaps. "Anna must know that there is no family greater than the one I offer."

He's going to kill my little girl. Not on my watch. As Dmitri has his back turned to me so he can pour another drink, I take my gun out of my holster and screw on the silencer. He turns to see me pointing my weapon at him. "You're not going to kill my daughter, Dmitri."

"What are you doing? You knew this day might come."

"I did, but she's my daughter, and no one lays a finger on my girl."

"What? Ilya, we're—"

I don't even let him finish the sentence. I put one bullet between his eyes. His head explodes and he collapses to the ground. I stand over his body, while I calculate my next move. I can't go to our regular cleaners, so I call the only person I can. "Yes," a male voice answers. This must be Agent.

"Patch me through to 15," I say. "Tell her it's Ilya."

He places me on hold for a moment before Anna answers. "Ilya." The easiness in her voice tells me she was expecting my call.

"I need a favor."

"What is it?"

"I need your cleaner."

"It's done?" She's clearly amused.

"It is."

"Is my sister safe?"

I inhale and chuckle. "As safe as she can be considering her job." There's a moment's pause where neither she nor I say anything. "15?"

"Leave. I'll take care of it. But I do have a question for you."

"What?"

"How involved was Agent in helping Dmitri?"

"Your Agent had nothing to do with us. We had our own man tracking him, which was difficult, and we could only get snippets of information but enough to piece together things about you."

"That stops now."

"Of course. And... thank..." Anna hangs up without another word. I look around the room and shake my head. "You should've left it alone," I say to Dmitri's lifeless body before turning and walking out of the room.

He had it coming.

Chapter Twenty-One

Adele

Sitting in Ben's office, I look at the reminders of him.

My phone rings, and I sigh, knowing it'll be Mom or Dad, if that's what I should even call them now. I glance over at the screen to see Dad's number. I've been avoiding him for a few days, and I'm not sure now is a good time to reopen the lines of communication.

I ignore the call, but he's insistent and tries again. And again. *And again.* I swipe to answer. "I'm not sure I want to talk to you."

"I understand, but there's something you need to know."

I stand and close the door to the office. "What?" I plonk back into the chair.

"Dmitri is dead." I don't even know how to respond to that. "Adele, did you hear me?"

"Yep." I swallow and tap my fingers on the table. "How did he die?"

"Someone shot him," he replies coldly.

"Was it Anna?"

"No, it wasn't."

"Do you know who it was?" I grind my teeth together as I await Dad's—*Ilya's*—answer. "Do you know who killed him?" I repeat.

"No, the others believe it was one of his enemies."

"What does this mean for the business?"

"It means it's up for grabs, but I've been earmarked. I'm the next logical selection for it."

My shoulders pull back as tears sting my eyes. "Which means I'll be hunting you."

"I'm not taking it, Adele. I don't want it."

I find myself smiling. "Then what are you going to do?"

"I'm retiring from the lifestyle."

"Is that even possible?"

"It is now Dmitri is gone. The reins will be handed over to the next in line after me."

"I guess you don't want to share that person's name with me, do you?"

"It's not Anna. She doesn't want anything to do with the business."

A humorless snicker vibrates in my chest. "I guess she has her own business." I open the top drawer of the desk and look at the phone that was delivered to me yesterday. "I'm glad, though."

"About Anna not taking over?"

"About you and Anna not being involved with the bratva. It'll make my job easier." I close the drawer again and roll my eyes. "Not sure how much easier considering my family's involvement in everything."

"I know you must be upset—"

"I'm not doing this with you now. One day soon, but not now. I need to clear my head and consider everything. I'd like to ask a favor of you and *Mom*," I say as I clear my throat.

"What is it?"

"For now, don't call me. I need to sort myself out, then I'll let you know how I fit into everything."

"Adele—"

"I need time," I interrupt. "I'm asking you to give me time. It's the least you owe me for a lifetime of deceit."

He clears his throat and whispers, "Of course. I love you."

"Bye." I hang up and place my phone back in the drawer beside the one Anna sent.

I sit back in the seat and place my hands on my head. Since Anna and Ben barged in and told me the truth about my true family, I've barely slept. My mind has been filled with questions about what I should do.

I swore to uphold the law and protect the people inside the borders of this country. I'm supposed to arrest criminals and see to it that they're brought to justice.

But how am I supposed to do that when my own sister is on the top ten list of wanted criminals, and my grandfather is—*was*—the head of the Russian mob? My entire life has been nothing but a series of lies. Even my birth mother was nothing more than an illusion.

To make matters worse, I have a meeting with Assistant Director Lomax tomorrow to determine my next assignment, and I really don't know what I'm going to do.

I should tell him about Anna, Ben, Ilya, and Dmitri. But, if I do, I know I'll be painted with the same brush as them after they use me to get Anna and Ben. I'll be implicated and investigated, and likely thrown out of the FBI.

If I don't tell him about them, then I'm allowing an assassin and an arms dealer to continue their work, essentially giving Anna and Ben immunity from the law.

I take Natalia's photo out of my pocket and shake my head as I stare at it. She was never a victim, she was by far the most selfish person I know. How could she abandon Anna, and then have me while she was addicted? I crinkle the photo in my hand, then straighten it out again. "Fuck you," I whisper as I tear the photo in half, then overlap the pieces and tear at them again. "You deserved exactly what you got," I spit toward the tiny pieces of the photo.

But now, this brings me back to Anna. I really don't know what I'm going to do. She pointed two guns at me and could've easily killed me. I don't have the ego to think I could've taken her on; I *know* what she's capable of. The problem is, I'm not sure I can turn her in. But if I don't, then I'm her accomplice.

She's my sister though, and she was brutally honest with me when my own family wasn't.

Jesus, I have a difficult decision to make, regardless of which way I go.

Either choice is wrong, yet right too. It'll be whichever decision I can live with.

Do I protect Anna, Ilya, and Ben or do I open myself up for scrutiny at work?

I let out a long breath and sit up in my seat. I have a deadline, and I guess I'll have to make my decision by tomorrow.

Fuck.

Epilogue

Anna

"Do you think Adele will turn you into the FBI?" I turn my neck and look at Ben, slightly shaking my head in answer to his question. "Why not? She can."

"Because, if she was going to do it, she would've done it already. She's had the phone for the past month," I snap at his irritating question.

"What's wrong with you?"

"I'm working, Ben, and you're asking me the stupidest of questions."

There's a small silence from Ben as I prepare for my next hit. "There's no way you can take the target at this distance," Ben comments as he lies beside me looking through his scope.

"Quarter turn to the left," I instruct.

"Target will appear in thirty seconds," Agent says through the comms. "Black SUV, the target is sitting in the center on the back seat."

"If you take the target out from here, it's over three miles."

"Can you shut up?" I say to Ben. "I need to concentrate." A tiny chuckle can be heard through the comms. "Agent," I warn.

"Sorry." I keep my focus as I continue to look through the scope. "Ten seconds." My finger hovers over the trigger. "Five, four, three…"

I see the black SUV approach and find my target through the scope. The woman in the back is on her phone. She's wearing oversized glasses and has a champagne flute in her hand. I take a breath, and depress the trigger.

The woosh of the bullet makes a distinctive sound as it slides through the chamber of my sniper rifle. I watch as the bullet finds its way to the SUV, shatters the front window, and explodes her head.

"Fuck me," Ben groans.

"Well done," Agent says.

"Confirm payment," I say as I remain lying on the rooftop.

Agent's fingers tap away on the keyboard. "Payment confirmed."

I hang up, then start disassembling the rifle. "One human trafficker down," Ben says.

"I don't even care that the human traffickers are killing each other for territory. It makes my job easier, and I'm being paid for it."

Ben helps me pack the rifle into the duffel bag. We head off the roof and down to where my car is parked. "Do you think I'll ever be able to hit a target from the distance you do?"

I look to Ben in disbelief. "No," I reply earnestly.

"Wow, don't sugar coat it for me, Anna. I can take the truth. Tell me what you really think."

"I did," I scoff. He's really been grating on my nerves lately.

We get to the car and I pop the trunk so Ben can place the duffel into it. "You have a way with words, don't you?"

"Do you want the truth, or do you want a lie?" I ask as I slide into the passenger seat and Ben enters the driver's seat.

"Can you spare my feelings just once?"

I huff and look out the window. "Sure," I say dryly. "With practice you'll be better than me," my voice is deadpan and almost robotic.

"What's gotten into you lately, you've been quite nasty."

"Nasty?" I ask as I bring my elbow up to lean on the window ledge and turn to stare at him. I *have* been particularly aggravated of late.

"Maybe nasty isn't the right word." I tilt my head and stare at him, blinking. "Maybe I know what it is."

"If you say anything about me being hungry, I'm going to beat the ever-living shit out of you."

Ben smirks as he clicks his tongue. "Well, you should have had breakfast before we left."

"I wasn't hungry."

"Which isn't like you. Do you want to stop and get something to eat? What do you feel like? Pizza?" My stomach churns at the thought of food. "No? What about Thai?" I screw my nose up. "Chinese?" Ugh. "Russian?" he asks with a laugh.

"Seriously?" I stare at him. "I'm not hungry."

"If it's not hunger, then it must be that time of the month," he says so carelessly. I lean over and punch him in the arm. "Hey, what was that for?"

"That time of the month? What a misogynistic thing to say."

"Well, you've been snappy."

"And that must mean I'm getting my period. Right?"

"If it's not that, it's because you've been working too hard. You've had eight hits in two weeks, Anna. *Eight.* And, six of them were all in different countries."

"Eight is nothing, I can do five a day and still be fine."

"Well...then." He swallows and lifts his chin. "You're either hungry or you're getting your period."

"I'm going to shoot you in the groin if you say that again."

"It's one or the other," he adamantly replies.

"I'm not hungry. And as far as my period is concerned, I'm due on the fourteenth, like every single month."

Ben shakes his head, then suddenly the car begins to slow. "The fourteenth?" Ben asks.

"Yes, the fourteenth," I reply with arrogance. "Like every other month."

"Anna, today is the twenty-second."

Wait, no that can't be right. I look around the car for my phone, and when I find it, I bring up the calendar. No, no, no. No! No. My heart is in my throat. This can't be happening. No, I refuse to believe it. I turn to Ben and whisper, "Fuck."

THE END

MARGARET MCHEYZER

Email: hit_149@yahoo.com

info@margaretmcheyzer.com

Facebook: Margaret McHeyzer Author

TikTok: Margaretmcheyzerauthor

Printed in Great Britain
by Amazon

26676529R00136